Gay Men (2 Books in 1)

The best sex stories for gay people who want to explore and act out their fantasies with their partner!

Explicit Erotic Sex Stories

Atreyu

(Gay)

High School lovers lose touch, re-find each other as adults

Pamela Vance

Part One

I met Teddy Atreyu - "Atreyu" to almost everyone who knew him - the first day of my freshman year in high school. Atreyu was the BMOC from get go. He looked older than the rest of us, and he had the bluest eyes any of us had ever seen. They were shockingly, almost frighteningly, blue. If I had not known differently, I'd have thought they were fake. They were that liquid. And, they danced when he smiled, which was almost all the time. Atreyu had a big, broad smile, framed by full, red lips. And, it was simultaneously knowing and mysterious. Atreyu may not have had a tiger by the tail, but he sure acted like he did.

For the next four years, he listened to music none of us had heard of, mixed drinks none of had tasted, and took drugs none of us could have gotten our hands on. And, he had whatever "it" is that makes people say "he has it." I do not know what that is, as I have never had "it." I have always been a little too furtive, a little too eager to please, a little too enthusiastic, a little too harried.

Atreyu was none of those things. He was casual, always seemed comfortable, languid almost, and never hurried. He sat back and soaked it all in. He moved slowly and surely. He seemed like he knew stuff none of us knew, like he had experienced things none of us had, or ever would.

For most of high school, I hovered near Atreyu's orbit. Both smart, we shared most classes. We studied together a little. We hung out together a little every now and then. We were friendly, but we were not really friends. I was the kind of person he nodded to in the hallway, not the kind of person he stopped to talk to.

Too many times, he caught me staring at him. Often, it was at his eyes. More often, it was at his body. Atreyu was a committed runner and weight lifter, and his body thickened, thinned, and developed throughout high school. While I stayed small and shapeless, he filled out beautifully. By the time we were 18 year old seniors, he was 6 feet tall, weighed 180 pounds, and had virtually no body fat. He was both muscular and lean. He had masculine hands and feet that he kept up properly. The only thing that separated him from Adonis was the mat of hair that covered his chest and the path that flowed from it into his pants. I loved that mat and that path. I desperately wanted to follow it. I hoped with all I was that he did not sense my desperation.

Spring semester of our senior year, the Honors German students who could afford it traveled for three weeks to Germany. In our group, there were three boys and nine girls. Once we got to

Frankfurt, we were joined by two groups from Minnesota, one from Blaine and one from Jackson. We shared the same bus and hotels for our three week trip.

The first night, we were in Rothenberg, a small village with a wall surrounding it. Atreyu asked me to walk the wall with him. I went. It was snowing and beautiful, and it took us a long time to circumnavigate the village. Our walk was oddly intimate, as we both talked, but also felt no need to fill the stillness with talk. It made no sense to that Atreyu had invited me, not his friend Steve or one of the girls who was pining for him. When the walk was over, Atreyu shook my hand.

"I really enjoyed that," he said as he smiled into me.

"Me, too," I responded as I smiled back.

By design, Frau Lucinda put me, Atreyu, and Steve in the same room that night. Surprisingly, the room had only a king bed, so we would be sleeping three across. Germany had no drinking age, so we were likely to be too drunk to care.

All of us went out. The German barkeepers responded to the American invasion with David Bowie's "This is not America." Atreyu drank German beer all night. I did not like beer, much less warm, bitter beer. So, I drank vodka and orange juice. Steve did not drink at all.

By the time we returned to the room, Atreyu and I were smashed. We both tugged off our shirts, pulled off our jeans, and collapsed onto the bed, wearing only our traditional white briefs. Steve climbed in to my right, leaving me in the middle.

Steve was objectively better looking than Atreyu. He was a long-distance runner, and he had long, sinewy muscles that were covered in light blonde hair. He also had a chiseled jaw beneath dark brown eyes and wavy blonde hair. When he was out of school, he looked like a surfer. When he was in school, he looked like a scion.

But, Steve never moved me the way Atreyu did. Steve just did not have "it." I would have blown him, but I was not hungry for him.

The hotel's steam heating system was banging away, and our room was hotter than Hades. Being drunk teenagers in Germany, we made lame gas chamber jokes and then laughed our asses off before passing out. When I woke up at 5 or so, I was covered in sweat. So, I kicked the covers off all of us. I immediately noticed that Atreyu had his right hand tucked into his white briefs and was holding his dick. I watched him the rest of the night, as every once and again he gripped and then released his hard on. The next day, everyone assumed I was hung over, and I probably was. But, mostly, I was tired from watching Atreyu squeeze and release his dick, when I should have gone back to sleep.

Two nights later, we were in a room with three twin beds. Only there were four of us: Me, Steve, Atreyu, and Katie, a blonde from Jackson. Katie was in bed with Atreyu. And, from the sound of it, she was having a good time. Atreyu had the decency to wait until he thought Steve and I were asleep, but I had only pretended to be. Not long after he whispered my name without answer, I heard Atreyu whisper "slip your panties off." Then, I heard some shifting around before Katie gasped, which I took to mean Atreyu's hard dick had entered her. The room was too dark for me to see exactly what was going on, but it was light enough that I figured out that Katie had her legs almost straight up in the air as Atreyu fucked her. As he did, her breathing quickened, and she started to make small, ragged noises. I gripped my own dick, imagining I was the one he was fucking. Listening to the slap of his dick slamming into her wet pussy, I was not going to last long. When Katie muttered "oh . . . oh . . . oh," I shot. When she whimpered "yes yes," I shot again. When Atreyu grunted, I could almost feel his orgasm building in my own balls, and I shot a third time. Atreyu collapsed onto Katie, exhaling loudly as he did. Before too long, she climbed out of the bed, and went to the bathroom to clean herself up. After she had, Atreyu rolled onto his side and stared in my direction. For some reason, I thought he was staring right at me, and that he knew I had jacked off to the sound of him fucking Katie. But, I hoped not.

The rest of the trip was pretty uneventful. We toured during the day, drank ourselves silly at night, and passed out drunk here and there, only to repeat the same general pattern the next day. It was that way in Salzberg. It was that way in Heidelberg. It was that way in Munich.

It was that way until the last night, in Frankfurt. That night, we stayed sober, as we had a very early flight home the next morning, and none of us were seasoned flyers. Hungover for an 8 hour flight seemed like a bad plan.

As we checked into our hotel room, we were beat from a trip of drunken debauchery. Our room had one full bed and one twin bed. Steve immediately claimed the twin, leaving Atreyu and me to share the full. When we climbed into bed in only our underwear, Atreyu did what he normally did, sliding his hand into his briefs and gripping his dick. I had to ask.

"What's the deal with that?"

"I like to hold my dick as I go to sleep."

"Every night?"

"Every night."

After Steve flipped the light out, Atreyu leaned his face close to my ear. "You can hold it tonight if you want."

I had no idea how to respond. I was gay, but I thought I was the only person in the world who knew that. I longed to touch a dick other than my own, but I feared the blowback if anyone ever found out I had. I was not the most popular kid in school, but I also was not an outcast. If people found out I was gay, then I would be. Gay was not okay at my high school, which was the kind of place that rewarded conformity and disdained difference of any kind. With all that swirling through my head in the split second I had to respond, I ignored Atreyu and pretended to be asleep. When I woke up, it was light, and Atreyu's hand was still in his underwear and holding his dick. I wondered if I had missed my chance.

Part Two

We caught our flight, and hopscotched our way back to our Missouri town. Neither Atreyu nor I mentioned our last night in Frankfurt, at least not until we were in Minnesota together later that summer.

During the remainder of our senior year, Atreyu and Katie kept in touch via long distance and letters (this was before cell phones, email, text messages, and snapchats). Mid-summer, Atreyu suggested a trip to Minnesota to "catch up" with (i.e. fuck) our friends.

Steve could not get off work, and we did not invite any of the girls to go. So, after work the Thursday before the 4th of July, he and I took my mother's featureless (no radio, no A/C) red Escort and started the 10 hour drive north to Jackson, MN. I had not seen Atreyu since graduation, almost two months before. Freed from our high school's grooming strictures, he had let his sandy blond hair grow long, and he had it pushed back behind his ears. His face was stubbly with whiskers. And, his eyes were the clear blue that comes with carelessness and rest. Years later, I realized he looked exactly like Curt Cobain would. He was hot. Sexy. Intoxicatingly so.

A few hours into the trip, I noticed that Atreyu's grey gym shorts were tenting. He noticed me noticing.

"Sorry. It happens when I am a car. I should have worn underwear."

"No worries."

I was driving, so I needed to keep my eyes on the road ahead. But, I found that virtually impossible, as I could see in the periphery Atreyu's hard dick down the right leg of his shorts. Periodically, he pushed down on it as hard as he could. It did not go down.

When we stopped for gas, he hopped out of the car and bounced inside, his hands covering his hard on. After pumping gas, I went to the bathroom. I saw his shoes under one of the stalls. From the slapping I could hear, it was clear he was jacking off, and pretty rapidly. I stayed at the urinal as long as I could, listening to him jerk his dick and his breath coming hard. I got hard as I listened. I left before he came, although I did not want to. I waited as long as long as I could, but I did not want to get caught.

When he got back in the car, he announced, "I should be alright now. At least for awhile." He smiled at me as I said it.

"Why?"

"You know. You just listened to me jack off."

I blushed crimson.

The rest of the drive to Jackson was tedious. As it got late, we both got very tired. We stayed awake by talking. Atreyu shared his life with me, both where he had been and where he wanted and thought he would go. He shared his secrets with me, both good and bad. And, I shared my life with him, both where I had been and where I hoped I was going. I also shared my secrets with him, including childhood secrets I had not shared with anyone else. I laid myself bare. It was way more intimate than I had been with anyone else, and way more intimate than I expected on a drive in an Escort to Minnesota. It was an echo to our walk around Rothenberg.

We rolled into Jackson well past midnight. We were staying at Cari's, and she put us in her divorced mother's room, where we would share her king-sized water bed. We were both beat, but it still took time to wind down. We continued talking. As we did, I noted that Atreyu had his hand in his briefs. As always. I fell asleep as we talked, imagining what he was feeling with that hand.

We slept long into July 3. When we awoke, we joined Cari in the kitchen, and Atreyu got a surprise. Katie, who he was looking to spend the weekend fucking, had a new boyfriend and so would be off-limits.

Still, Katie joined the rest of our friends at Cari's that afternoon for a pool party. Atreyu was surly from the get go. He clearly wanted to get laid, and he was pissed he was misled into driving 10 hours only to be thwarted.

I, on the other hand, was having a blast. It was July 3rd, it was only 80 degrees, there was an unlimited supply of beer, and the boys were mostly naked, showing off their muscled chests, perfect nipples, and rippled stomachs. I spent most of the day in the water. I barely saw Atreyu.

Having started very early, the party broke up when everyone got hungry. Cari grilled burgers for the small group of us left over, which included her, me, Atreyu, and Darryl, a somewhat unkempt dude who seemed cool as shit. After the burgers and a few more beers, Cari and Darryl joined hands and headed into the house. It was obvious they were going to fuck. Their exit left me and Atreyu poolside, alone.

"Do you smoke?" he asked.

"No, my mom smokes, and it has always grossed me out. I can't stand the things."

"Pot, dork. Not cigarettes."

"Oh. No, I never have."

"Wanna try?"

"I dunno. I kind of thought that was something I would never do."

"Suit yourself, but you live only once. At least, that is what they teach us. I have nothing on my list of 'something I would never do.' I want to do it all."

With that, Atreyu stood up, walked to the shallow end of the pool, dangled his legs over the edge, and lit a joint. He raised it to his mouth and inhaled deeply. As far as I could tell, he never exhaled.

I stood up, adjusted my trunks, walked the length of pool, and sat down next to him. I touched my foot to his as I dangled my legs in the water. He did not pull his foot away. Instead, he offered me the joint again.

"Just try it, dork."

"What do I do?"

"Hold it to your mouth, suck in as deeply as you can, and then hold your breath for as long as you can."

I tried. I choked and coughed almost instantly, expelling the smoke almost as fast I tried to take it in. Atreyu laughed, his smile illuminating his crazy blue eyes.

"Here, I'll help you."

He put the joint backward in his mouth, put his hand on the back of my head, and moved his face toward mine. For some reason, I opened my mouth, and he put the small end of the joint in my mouth. When I closed my mouth, our lips touched. He blew out, and my mouth filled with smoke. I started to swallow, but then stopped and just breathed in, as deeply as I could. I felt the smoke fill me. I held it as long as I could. I wanted to exhale, but my lips were still pressed to his, and I was not about to pull away. We were not kissing, but we were also not not kissing. He opened his eyes and looked into mine. I looked back, deeply. I held the look as long as I could, before I finally pulled away, choking.

"Congratulations on your first shotgun, dork."

"Thanks, I guess."

Atreyu took another long drag off the joint and handed it to me. I dragged back, coughing again, violently. Soon, the joint was almost gone, and he pulled out another.

"Let's move to the deck."

"Okay."

We stood, pulling our legs out of the pool. We walked to the deck and plopped down in two lounge chairs. He dragged and then passed me the joint. I dragged and passed it back. He put the lit end in his mouth and leaned over for another shotgun. I moved my face to meet his, and I put my hand around the back of his neck. I made sure we were lip to lip before he delivered my second shotgun. I took it all in, as deeply as I could. Our lips remained together. He pulled away, removed the joint, said "blow it back," and put his mouth back to mine. I opened my mouth a little, and blew the smoke back into his. He inhaled it. He pulled back and held it in. Our faces were close. He leaned forward, I opened my mouth, and he blew what remained of the smoke back into my mouth. I was titillated. And rock hard.

We finished the joint like that, trading smoke back and forth and back and forth. When the joint was gone, he got up, walked away, and returned with two vodkas. Mine burned the shit out of me, high or not. He sipped his, casually, coolly.

We both laid back in our chairs, totally relaxed, staring at the equally dark and starry sky. Neither of us spoke.

I was both drunk and high. I suspected he was, too. I am not sure I had ever been more relaxed.

"Let's swim."

"Okay."

He stood up and pulled his trunks off as he walked toward the pool. The moon lit his ass as his hips swung. Nude when he got to the pool, he jumped in. I followed, jumping in with my trunks still on.

"Have you ever skinny dipped?"

"Nope."

"Take your trunks off. Being naked in the water is awesome."

"I'm okay."

"Take your trunks off, dork."

I swam to the shallow end and did as I was told, dumping my trunks on the edge of the pool. Then, I turned and swam back toward him. He was right. Swimming nude was awesome. I felt completely free, the water caressing my dick and balls. We treaded water in the deep end for awhile. When I got tired, I swam to the side, and rested the back of my head against it, my arms spread wide beside me. Atreyu followed me. He grabbed the side of the pool, his hands on either side of me. He was right in front of me. He had me trapped. He stared at me and smiled. I stared back for as long as I could, smiling back at him. I finally looked away. I was rock hard.

"Let's go inside."

"Are you sure? It's fantastic out here." I stalled. I did not want to climb out of the pool with a hard on he was sure to see.

"I'm sure." He moved to the side and pulled himself out of the pool, exposing his beautiful ass as he did. When he was out, I swam to the shallow end, clambered out as fast as I could, and wrapped a towel around me in a futile attempt to conceal my rock hard dick. Atreyu walked toward me from the other end of the pool. He, too, was rock hard, but he did not care that I saw it. He seemed to want me to see it. He seemed to be flaunting it.

I had not seen his dick hard before. It was awesome. As suspected, he was a shower. His dick was big and thick and pretty, curving gently up. I wanted it. More than I had ever wanted anything.

He picked his towel up, wrapped it around his neck, and walked toward the house, his dick leading the way and his ass swaying in front of me. I followed.

When we got to the room, Atreyu moved toward his gym bag, dug out a pair of briefs, and tugged them on. When he turned around, it was clear his dick was still hard, sticking up and to the right, with the head visible above the elastic band. He smiled at me, turned, and went into the bathroom. As he brushed his teeth, I dropped my towel, put on a pair of boxers, and pulled on an undershirt. I could not sleep shirtless.

When Atreyu finished in the bathroom, I took my turn. I washed my face, brushed my teeth, and - just in case - smelled my arm pits. They were fine. I turned out the light and returned to the room. Atreyu was sitting on the bed, his back to the headboard and the sheet draped over his crotch.

I climbed into the bed, jostling him with the "waves" I created. Once in, I sat like he was, as close to him as I could without being too obvious.

"Are you high?" he asked.

"Yep."

"Me, too. But, I could go a little higher."

With that, he lit another joint and sucked in as much as he could. He offered it to me, but I declined. I had had all the pot I thought I should. After another couple drags, Atreyu licked his finger, extinguished the joint, and returned it to his "fun bag."

We sat in silence against the tufted headboard. After a bit, he looked over at me and smiled.

"How's your high, dork?"

"I am having a very good time."

"Me, too." He paused. "My only problem is pot gives me the munchies. And makes me horny."

"I can help with at least one of those." I got up, went to the kitchen, and returned with an open bag of Chips Ahoys. We quickly devoured the dozen or so that were left.

"I'm still horny as hell."

I flashed back to Frankfurt. I may have missed my chance there. I did not want to miss it again, but I was helpless and hopeless as to what to do. I turned my head toward him. He smiled at me, and I noticed his right hand was on his dick, and it was hard, partially out of his briefs, and pointed straight at his navel.

He beat me to it.

"You want to help with this, too?"

I froze. "Uh, I don't think so."

"C'mon, you have been staring at me for four years, you watched me fuck that chick in Laposky's room, you jerked off while I fucked Katie, and you listened to me jack off just yesterday. You definitely want to help me."

"I am not gay."

"I did not say you were, and I do not care if you are. I just want to get off, and I'd prefer you do it. But, I can do it myself."

"Fire away."

With that, he raised his hips, pulled down his briefs, and started to stroke his long, thick dick right in front of me. I should not have stared, but I did. I could not not stare.

"Last chance," he offered.

I stared at his dick. It was awesome, lengthened to 8+ inches, thicker than my wrist, and curved toward his navel.

My throat was too dry to speak, so I just reached for his dick, tentatively. Atreyu pulled his hand away and let me take it. It was thicker than it looked. It was hot to my touch. As I watched my hand move up and down, he pulled my head toward his hairy chest and pressed me tightly to it. When he released the pressure, I licked his right nipple gently, then eagerly started sucking it. At the same time, I continued to jerk his thick dick. Before long, his breath became ragged, and I could feel his orgasm build in his throbbing dick. When I bit his nipple, he came in white arcs. The first hit his chin and neck. The next two hit his chest. The next hit his stomach. And, the last dribbled out of his bulbous head onto my hand.

I could not believe it. I had just swum naked with and then jacked Teddy AAtreyu. I had gone higher, too.

I wanted to taste his cum, but I feared he would think me freakish - and gay - if I did. So, I just lay with my head on his chest, still holding his softening dick.

"That was awesome. Did you enjoy it?

"I did."

"You could have done all of that in Frankfurt."

"I thought maybe. But, I did not know."

"I said, 'you can hold it tonight if you want.' How were you confused?"

"I thought maybe it was a trap."

"Do you feel trapped now?"

"No, not at all."

We sat in silence for awhile. He broke the silence, "I'm beat. I will see you in the morning." With that, he turned his back to me, fluffed his pillow, and settled in to sleep, his hairy chest and stomach still covered with his cum. I moved to my side and did the same, my back to him. Before falling asleep, I licked and sucked his dry cum off my hand. It was delicious.

Part Three

The next day was the 4th. Again, Atreyu and I slept in. When we awoke, he was still naked, and we were both sporting "morning wood." Atreyu spit in his hand, grabbed his dick, and started stroking it. I looked from his dick to his face. He was looking back at me, smiling.

When he started jerking harder, I moved toward him. Leaning on my left arm, I grabbed his balls with my right hand and started playing with them. He spread his legs a little. As I continued to play with his balls, he quickened his hand on his dick, and spread his legs farther apart.

He raised his hips. "Play with my ass." Not certain what he meant, I started rubbing his ass cheeks.

"Play with my asshole, dork."

"Oh."

Not sure how to, I rubbed his sphincter up and down with one finger like I had rubbed Cathi Summers' pussy in 10th grade. It must have been right, as he let out a light moan and jerked his dick harder.

"Finger me."

"What?"

"Finger me. Lick your finger, and stick it in my ass."

I was vexed, but I did what I was told. My finger tasted funky when I put it in my mouth, but it was not really a bad funky. I coated it with spit, reached down, and pushed the tip into his ass.

"Go a little deeper."

I did as directed, pressing my finger into the first knuckle.

"Don't be shy. Push it all the way in."

I did as he requested. His ass was warm and smooth, almost velvety. I am not sure what I expected, but this was not it. I swirled my finger around. Before long, he gasped as his ass clenched and he shot a string of cum onto his face and neck, then two more strings onto his chest, and yet another string onto his stomach. It was almost the same load as the night before.

I kept my finger where it was, feeling his orgasm from the inside. Watching and feeling him come was too much, and I came in my boxers without even touching myself. I do not know whether Atreyu knew I had.

When we had both calmed down, he caught me looking at the splattering of cum caught in the hair on his chest and stomach. Smiling at me, he took his right hand, scooped a healthy portion onto his index finger, and slipped his finger into his mouth, his brilliant blue eyes fixed on mine the whole time. He sucked his finger, then swallowed his own cum, smiling. Then he said "thanks," rocked off the water bed, and headed to the shower. I threw myself back on the bed and tried to figure out just what was going on.

Part Four

The 4th of July was much like the 3rd. Cari's pool was packed with mostly 18 year old kids who did not have a care in the world, except maybe that we would run out of beer. From the number of coolers poolside, that seemed unlikely.

I loved water, so I spent most of the day in the pool, swimming with and talking to friends and to Philip, Katie's new boyfriend. Philip was pretty, much as Matt Bomer is pretty today. You know the type: teeth a little too white and straight, hair a little too styled, jaw a little too chiseled. He was a little like a flavored beer. At first glance, he was tasty. But, the more you looked, the more cloying he became.

I had not seen Atreyu for over an hour or so. Just as I noticed his absence, he returned to the pool area. I could tell from the look on his face that he had been up to no good. He slid into the pool next to me. He reeked of pot.

"Where've you been?"

"Smoking . . . and fucking."

"Fucking?" A knot balled in my stomach. "Who?"

"That pretty boy's girlfriend. While you were fucking around with him in the water, I was fucking her in the water . . . bed."

He had smiled widely as he paused, presumably for dramatic effect.

The knot in my stomach tightened. I am not sure what I thought was going on, but the idea that he had fucked Katie in "our" bed upset me terribly. I fought back tears until I had to slip underwater to hide them. I stayed down as long as I could. Before I drowned myself, I swam across the pool, pulled myself out of the water, and headed off. I did not look back.

I needed to clear my head, so I went for a slightly drunken run. I knew Atreyu and I were not boyfriends, but I also did not expect him to have sex with me in the morning and then a girl in the afternoon. Not that we had really had sex. We had not kissed. He had not touched me. I had basically serviced him. Actually, I had basically done only what he told me to do.

I avoided Atreyu when my run was over, and I turned in not long after the guests had left. Atreyu did not join me for a long time. Still, I was wide awake when he came into the room, stripped to his briefs, and climbed into bed.

"You awake?" he asked.

"Yes."

"What was today about?"

"I don't really want to talk about it."

"I do, dork. So talk."

"Fine. At first, I was hurt that you had hooked up with Katie. I felt betrayed, which I now realize was totally fucked up. I think I was thinking that what we did last night and this morning meant more than it did. I think I let my imagination get ahead of the facts. During my run, I realized I was being ridiculous. We had not done anything last night or this morning. I had basically serviced you. When I realized that, I started feeling a bit used."

"I thought you weren't gay."

"I'm not."

"And, used? I had offered myself to you when we were in Germany. I thought you would enjoy it, and I was curious about you."

"I'm over it."

"You don't seem like it."

"Well, I am."

We lay there in silence for awhile. I felt ridiculous.

I broke the uncomfortable silence. "You got any more pot?"

"Nope, I finished it all off about 20 minutes ago outside." After a pause, "I have something else, though."

"What?"

"A pill. Ecstasy. You want one?"

"What does it do?"

"A lot. It makes you bounce."

I needed a mood changer. I held my hand out. He did not give me the pill. Instead, he put it on his tongue and lowered his mouth to mine. I grimaced.

He pulled back, removed it briefly, and said, "This is how it's done. Take it, dork."

He replaced it and came back toward me. I took it, our tongues touching as I did. My resolve evanesced with the touch.

I felt nothing for some time. We leaned against the headboard staring forward and breathing. Just when I thought I was immune to the effects of X, a feeling of peace and warmth overwhelmed me. Atreyu followed right behind me.

He looked at me. "Are you there?"

"I am."

"Awesome, in't it?"

"Yep."

With that, he leaned toward me, whispered "sorry about today," and placed his mouth on mine. I was totally caught off guard. As he opened his mouth, I did, too, and our tongues touched again. A jolt shot through me. I had heard from girls that Atreyu was our school's best kisser. I doubt any of them had kissed him while X'ing. Jolts kept shooting through me as our tongues danced. His lips were full but firm. His tongue was wet but not sloppy. He sucked my tongue, nibbled at it, and sucked it some more. It was the most perfect kiss, and it did not seem like it was ever going to end. Just when I thought I would rather pass out than break that kiss, he pulled back.

"I hope that makes up a little bit for what you were feeling. Now, take your clothes off."

"What?"

"Get naked, dork," he insisted as he tugged on my boxers.

"Are you going to take yours off?"

He answered by standing on the bed, pulling down his briefs, and stepping out of them. Jostled by the water bed, he lost his footing and fell on me.

"Hi there," he said, as he moved over me and kissed me again. He hooked the band of my boxers in both his hands and tugged them them down as he did. I broke the kiss, but only to pull my undershirt over my head. He got up, stood at the end of the bed, pulled my boxers the rest of the way off, and then pulled me flat by my feet. Standing at the foot of the bed, he cupped he slid his dick between my feet and pretended to fuck them. His dick was slick with precum, and his thrusting slicked my feet with it. When he stopped, he bent down and licked the stickiness off my feet. I was ticklish, and I had never had anyone lick my feet before. The sensation was only enhanced by the X. It was torture, and I squirmed so much I feared I might kick his face.

Just when I thought I could not take anymore, he stopped and started to crawl up me, licking my calves, then my thighs.

When he got to my rock hard dick, he stopped. I was neither as long nor as thick as he was, but I was also not small. My "little boy dick" was now an average sized "man dick."

He took what I had in his mouth, going all the way to the base. I could not believe what was happening. I felt like I was on fire, and I knew I would not last long. As he sucked me, he grabbed my balls with his right hand and squeezed. I felt my orgasm start to build in his hand.

"I'm gonna come," I pleaded.

He kept right on sucking, taking me deeper and faster as he did.

"I'm gonna come," I warned, more insistently. When he did not stop, I unloaded in his mouth. He swallowed and kept going. I unloaded again and again. Each time, he swallowed and kept going. I was drained and hyper-sensitive, but he just kept going until I had to force him to stop.

He resumed his trek, licking his way up the rest of my body. I tingled from head to toe. When he sucked my left nipple, I almost could not bear it. When he licked under my arms, I almost cried out.

He kept coming. He licked my clavicle. Then, he licked my neck. My neck is naturally sensitive. On X, my neck was super-sensitive. I cringed.

He kept coming. He sucked my chin. He kissed my eyes. Then, he planted his mouth on mine. He took my breath away, plunging his tongue into my mouth, grabbing my tongue with his teeth, and sucking it back into his mouth. As he did, I gripped his ass and forced his hard dick into my soft one. I felt like I was under a waterfall.

He kept going, sliding up me until he was kneeling in front of my face. I took his beautiful dick into my mouth. He curved the wrong way for the angle, but he did not seem to mind. He moaned, grabbed the back of my head, and started fucking my mouth. I grabbed his hips and tried to control his thrusts. I could not, but he settled into a tolerable rhythm. It was hard to tell whether I was sucking his dick or he was fucking my face. I did not care. I was tumbling.

His pace quickened. I tried to devour him. He grabbed my head with both his hands. I hungrily met him. He drove himself in as far as he could. With my hands on his ass, I tried to drive him deeper.

I thought I would gag. He drove deeper. I felt full. He pulled back, and then he drove deeper still.

My dick was hard as a rock. I grabbed it with my right hand, still using my left hand to control his depth.

He came hard. I gagged on his cum, and some ran out of my mouth. I recovered and swallowed just in time to receive another shot. I swallowed again.

I came. Hard. It hit his back and ass. He shot again. I swallowed again, easily. I shot, again hitting his backside. He shot again, and I did, too. We both kept coming until we could not come any more.

Spent, he sat back on my hips, exhaled deeply, and lowered his head to my left shoulder. I held his head with both hands. Then, I ran my hands down his back, smearing my cum. I brought my hand to my mouth and tasted myself. He lowered his face to mine, licked his cum off my cheek, and kissed me deeply. Our cum mixed as he did.

I adjusted myself so I was flat. He lowered himself onto me, then raised up, staring into my eyes. I smiled. He smiled back. Then, he lowered his mouth to mine and kissed me some more. I hungrily kissed back. I hooked my legs around his. We kissed and kissed and kissed.

"I am not using you."

"I know."

He kissed again.

"Can I fuck you?"

"I dunno. Can I fuck you?"

"If I can fuck you first, dork."

I hesitated. "Deal."

"I need to rest a little first."

"Me, too."

He rolled off of me and we lay on the bed side by side. The moon through the window illuminated his hairy chest. I rolled onto my side and started to run my hands through his chest hair and down his trail. I started at his left nipple, moved to the right, moved to his navel, and then moved to his dick. He hardened.

"Raise your arm." He put his arms behind his head, revealing hairy, hollow pits. I buried my face in his left pit as I continued to play with his dick and balls. I inhaled deeply. He smelled of chlorine, sweat, and sex. I inhaled deeply again. The combination of smells was intoxicating. Then, he pulled me to him. He was hard in my hand. I was hard against his leg.

"Let's fuck," he insisted

He rolled off the bed, walked to his bag, and returned with condoms and lube. He gave me the condom, so I tore it open with my teeth, and rolled it onto his hard dick. I had never put a condom on myself, much less on someone else. It was hot.

He lubed his dick and then told me to roll over. I did. Before I knew what was happening, he spread my ass checks and lowered his face to my asshole. He started rimming me. I thought I might combust. I wanted him to stop. I wanted him never to stop. I wanted to scream. I wanted never to make another noise.

I did not have to decide what to do. Before I did, his tongue penetrated me, and he ate my ass hard. While he pushed in, I pushed back. I was a virgin. Still, the sensation made me hungry for him.

"Fuck me," I insisted.

"Be patient. I have to get you ready." He squirted a glob of lube in my ass crack, then used his fingers to prepare me. It was uncomfortable, but I was needy for what it portended.

He licked his way back up until he was on my back. He whispered, "Help me in."

I reached behind me, grabbed his dick, and placed him at my opening. His head was next to mine. I turned to him, and he kissed me hard.

I said "Go."

He pushed hard. I naturally resisted, but he forced his head in. I feared it would hurt a lot, but it was not as bad as I feared. Maybe the X softened it all.

I was about to burst. "Go."

He lowered his hands to my hips, told me to take a deep breath (I did), and pushed. I inhaled deeply as he slid in. I am not sure I have ever felt that full. It felt like he was in my throat.

"Shhhh. Take a deep breath and relax."

Both are easier said than done, especially when you have a dick in your ass for the first time. I breathed as deeply as I could and held it. I tried to imagine I was relaxed. I was not.

"I'm sorry, but I can't hold back."

He pulled out and pushed back in, slowly, again and again. It ached. Then, it didn't.

He started fucking me in earnest. He raised himself up on his arms for leverage, then pushed my legs apart with his knees. He started to go faster, fucking me like an animal, and I wanted him to stop. Then, I wanted him to fuck me harder. Then, I wanted him to fuck me forever. Then, I wanted to watch his face as he came inside me.

"Stop," I demanded, as he dripped sweat on my back and ass.

"What?"

"Stop. I want to watch you."

I forced him out of me and flipped over. He was wet with sweat. He smiled as I guided him back inside me. He leaned down and kissed me as he started to fuck me again. I have never felt more vulnerable or more invulnerable.

"I am about to come."

"Come on my face." I had no idea where that came from.

He pulled out, ripped the condom off, arched his back, and used his hand to come at me. Some hit my face. Most hit my chest and stomach. I gathered what hit my face and ate it. He continued to stroke his dick. To my surprise, he announced, "I'm coming again."

I slid forward and took the head of his dick in my mouth. He shot, and I swallowed it all. When he was done, he collapsed onto his side. I positioned myself next to him, and kissed him.

"I can taste myself."

"You taste awesome."

"So do you." He closed his eyes, like he was going to go to sleep. But, we were not finished.

"I still get to fuck you." I moved my face toward his, and we kissed a kiss that poets write about. It was simultaneously tender and hungry and gentle and reckless. It took his fatigue away. He rolled me on top of him.

"Grab the condom off the nightstand and put it on me."

"You don't need it."

"At least get me the lube."

"You don't need that, either."

He spit in his hand, and rubbed it on my dick. He spit in his hand again, and rubbed it on his asshole. Then, he grabbed my dick and lined me up. I pushed, and he opened to me. A neophyte, I did not know how to control myself, and I went all the way in. He gasped and said, "Hold it right there. Give me a little time to get used to this."

After a bit, he raised his legs higher, grabbed my ass, and said, "okay, now fuck me." I did as he demanded, forcing myself into him as deeply as I could. He used his hands on my ass to control my pace. When he was ready, he removed them, and I naturally speeded up. I started panting. So did he. I started sweating. So did he. I could not last. I had never fucked anyone.

"I'm about to come."

"Don't pull out. Come inside me."

With a deep thrust, I came and came, filling him. He was jerking his own dick, and he came, too, splashing cum all over his stomach.

Smiling at him, I lowered myself and ate as much cum off his stomach as I could. With his cum still on my tongue, I kissed him. He devoured me, clamping my face to his with his hands. We kissed and kissed and kissed some more. He pulled his head from mine.

"We need to sleep. We have a long drive tomorrow."

He turned off the light and turned back toward me. He was on his right side, I was on my left, and we were sharing a pillow. Our faces were close. I moved enough that our lips were touching. We fell asleep kissing.

Part Five

When I woke up, Atreyu was holding me, his morning wood right between my ass cheeks. He kissed my neck and rubbed my chest. He rolled away, I heard a tube click open, and he was back. He pushed his left hand between my ass checks, smearing it with wetness. His dick pushed against my ass. He wanted to fuck me again, and I wanted him to fuck me again. I rolled over on my stomach, and raised up on all fours. He scrambled behind me and pushed his dick at me. Without the X to cushion it, the penetration hurt like hell. I thought I was going to cleave in two. He forced himself all the way in. He stayed there. When he felt me relax, he pulled out slowly, then pushed back in just as slowly. He knew what he was doing. He reached around and took me in his hand. The pain started to ebb and was replaced with the dual pleasure of him simultaneously stroking my ass and my dick. Sweat broke out all over my body. I was close. He slammed into me as deeply as he could. As he did, he said "oh fuck." He was coming. The feeling of him coming inside me was too much, and I came also. He slowly fucked his last drops into me, and slowly jerked my last drops out of me. I collapsed onto the bed, and he fell on top of me. He licked my cum off his hand, then turned my head so he could kiss me. I tasted myself in the kiss. He pulled back.

"Good morning."

"Good morning."

"It's almost 9. We need to get going."

We loaded the Escort and headed back to Missouri. As we drove, I confessed "I have never done any of that before."

"I have."

"No kidding."

"I like sex. . . .A lot."

"You're good at it."

"Practice makes perfect."

"Actually, practice make permanent, not perfect."

"You really are a dork."

"Guilty. But, where did you get practice?"

"I do not discuss such things. You shouldn't either."

45

"Have you practiced with a lot of guys?"

"I do not discuss such things. You shouldn't either."

He anticipated my confusion about what was going on.

"I am not going to be your boyfriend. But, we can fuck around until we head off to college next month."

"Who said I wanted a boyfriend?"

He looked at me and smiled. I could get lost in that smile. I definitely wanted a boyfriend. And, he knew it.

He took the first shift driving. About three hours into the trip, I noticed he was hard, his dick again extended down the right leg of his grey gym shorts. He noticed me noticing.

"You should have worn underwear."

"They'd have gotten in the way."

"Of what?"

Without answering, he pulled the leg of his shorts up, exposing his hard dick. "I thought maybe you'd blow me while I drive, dork."

I was thrilled. I unbuckled my seat belt, adjusted my position, and took his dick into my mouth. I added my right hand as an extension of my mouth. I started working his dick.

"Slow down. It's a long drive."

I did as instructed. I sucked the head of his dick, lolling it around in my mouth and teasing it with my tongue. I took as much of him as I could in my mouth, slowing moving up and down the shaft of his dick. I savored it.

"This is going to be hard without cruise control," he offered.

As I mentioned earlier, my mother's Escort had no features. It was like a Flintstone car, only with a combustible engine. It was a coke can with wheels.

I pulled off his dick. "When you get close, just pull over."

"Nope. Part of the thrill is to come while driving."

"Don't kill me."

"I won't."

I took him back in my mouth. Like him, I had no desire for the blow job to end. I wanted to suck him as long as I could. I loved the feel of him in my mouth, and I loved the control I had over him.

"That feels great. Just keep doing what you're doing. I will let you know if I want to come." He started playing with my hair.

I have no idea how long I sucked his dick. It seemed like a long time. My side started to ache. So did my jaw. I pulled off and sat up.

"I need a break."

"That's fine." He looked at me and smiled. It was a perfect smile. His eyes danced above it. I smiled back.

"But don't take too long. I want to come in your mouth again."

I did not hesitate. I leaned over and took him back in my mouth. I worked him hard. I felt him strain to meet me. I had a perfect grip on him with my mouth. I sucked as hard as I could.

"Jesus Christ, here it comes," he gasped as he filled my mouth. I swallowed and kept going. He unloaded again. I swallowed again and kept going. He unloaded again to a ragged "Oh my God." I swallowed and kept going. I wanted to drain him, and I did.

"You have to stop."

I pulled off. "I thought maybe you would come again."

"Not this time. But, that was awesome. You can do that whenever you want."

"I doubt that. We would die of starvation and sleep deprivation."

"Maybe. But, what a way to go out."

Part Six

We talked for the next 7 hours. We laughed, sympathized, and empathized. This was more than two 18 year old boys swapping stories. It was intimate. It was love. When we stopped at a diner to eat, he sat on the same side of the booth as I did. He pressed his leg against mine under the table. I felt euphoric. I felt afraid.

When we drove back into our town, it was late and dark, I knew all there was to know about Atreyu, and he knew all there was to know about me. Atreyu had driven the entire way, and he was beat. He pulled into his driveway, turned the car off, and threw his head back against the seat.

"When do you leave for school?" he asked.

"August 26. You?"

"Same. So, we have about six weeks."

"For what?"

"Us."

Those two letters hung in the air. I wanted to grab them, but they were too surprising and alien. So, I watched them float, wondering if they meant more than I thought or less than I hoped. There was no "us" if all we were doing was "fucking around."

Atreyu got out of the car, so I did, too. We met at the hatchback. He popped it open and grabbed his bag. I slammed it back shut.

"Okay, then," he said.

"Yes, okay then," I responded.

He threw his bag over his shoulder and pulled me to him, kissing me hard on the mouth. I kissed him back. His arms were around my shoulders, and my arms were around his waist.

When he pulled away, he said, "Great trip, dork. Call me when you wake up in the morning."

"Okay," I responded, simply and unelegantly.

I missed the next morning, sleeping well past noon. When I awoke, I could not piece the trip together. Atreyu apparently had known all along that I was watching him and wanting him. When I had the chance, I took drugs with him, betraying what I thought I was, and I slept with him, revealing who I knew I was. I could not figure out what was going on. He said he did not want to be my boyfriend, but it sure felt like that's what he was, and what he wanted. I felt like a feather in a whirlwind. I also felt wide open and vulnerable. And, I hate that feeling.

My natural instinct toward self-preservation kicked in. I got up. I resisted the urge to call him, as he had directed. Instead, I went to the basement and lifted weights. When I was done, I showered and ate a light "breakfast." I had no reason to be here or there. I was hanging around. It was pouring down rain, almost sideways, the way it rains in the summer in the midwest. I laid on my bed and watched it pour through my bedroom window, dozing in and out of sleep and mindlessly thumbing through a book.

The doorbell rang. When I answered it, Atreyu stood there, soaking wet.

"You didn't call."

"I forgot," I lied.

"Can I come in?"

"Sure," I said, stepping aside.

We walked to my room. "We need to get you out of those wet clothes."

"I thought you'd never ask." He smiled at me. It was an "I get whatever I want" smile. He always won, and he knew it.

I tossed him a shirt and shorts. "Give me your wet clothes. I will put them in the dryer." He stripped. He picked up the shirt and shorts I had tossed him and carelessly threw them in the corner.

I picked up his wet clothes and headed to the basement. When I returned to my room, Atreyu was on my bed, naked, and hard. His arms were behind his head, and he was smiling broadly. He was beautiful, and I was lost.

"What took you so long?"

"Get dressed."

"Get undressed."

I locked my door and leaned against it. I was too weak to say no, but too vulnerable to say yes. I closed my eyes and sighed.

Atreyu got up and moved to me. When he took my face in his hands, I opened my eyes. Whispering "hey, dork," he kissed me. I kissed him back. We kissed for some time. As we did, Atreyu removed my clothes.

I needed clarity. "What is this?"

"It's us."

Those two letters again.

We moved to the bed. Our hands were all over each other. Our mouths were, too. We kissed and licked and sucked and grabbed and tugged and squeezed. We were soon inverted. We sucked each other eagerly. We were locked together, mimicking each other's movements. Our torsos rubbed together. Our hands were on each other's asses, pulling the other deeper. into our mouths. We were together, matching the other's movements. As we moved closer to the edge, we continued in lockstep. We came at the same time, each gripping the other's ass hard and sucking as hard as we could. We drank each other, trying desperately to take in as much of the other as possible.

Spent, we pulled apart. We laid head to toe. He reached his arm toward me, and my hand met his. We lay like that, our right hands intertwined. I rolled onto my right side and put my head to his left foot. He mirrored me. We were now perfectly head to toe. We licked each other's feet. We sucked each other's toes.

"Come up here," he asked.

I did as requested. When we were head to head, he pulled my face to his, and we kissed deeply. He wrapped his arms around me and pulled me as close as he could. We were pressed together every where we could be. I pulled back, and looked into his crystalline eyes. He looked as deeply into mine. He kissed me again, keeping his eyes open. I kissed him back, keeping my eyes open and staring into his.

"The next time I tell you to call me, call me."

"Why? If I had, I would have missed that."

I fell asleep with my head in his chest. We were nude and happy and, his cautionary words notwithstanding, lost in each other. We were boyfriends. I knew it.

Part Seven

We spent the next six weeks like that, together every chance we had. It felt like a tornado, spinning out of control. We fell, hard, with only our impending separation to blight our careless, youthful lives. We were wildly in love, as only teenagers could be. I delighted when he was there, and I ached when he was not. I was incapable of perspective.

As our last weekend together approached, Teddy - what I now called him, as "Atreyu" seemed too common - suggested we go away. I agreed. We made reservations at the Chase Park Plaza. We checked in on Friday afternoon. We had tickets to the Cardinals' game that night. Once we were checked in, we had just enough time to fool around before heading to the game. As had become our general pattern, Teddy topped me. I loved the feel of him inside me, the weight of him on top of me, the ragged breathing when he came, the smile on his face when he recovered. As I often did, I came when he did, without touching myself.

The game was awesome. Teddy conned a vendor into selling us beer. The Redbirds won in dramatic fashion. By the time the game was over, we were drunk and delirious. Instead of going out, we headed back to our hotel. We could feel the clock ticking, and we wanted to be alone together. Unlike that afternoon, our post-game celebration was slow and steady. I edged closer and closer and then had him back off. He edged closer and closer and then backed off. By the time he was ready to come, we were both dripping with sweat. We had almost perfected our sex, so we came together, him inside me, and me all over myself. Exhausted, he collapsed onto me, mixing our sweat with my cum. I wrapped my arms around him. He buried his face in my neck. I gave in.

"I love you, Teddy." Neither of us had ventured there before.

He pulled his head back and surprised me. "I love you, too, dork. A lot."

We fell asleep like that. I woke up about an hour later, cold. He eased off me, and I pulled the comforter up over us. I buried my face in his chest, he slid his leg between mine, and we fell back asleep, loving each other.

The next day, we went to the zoo. St. Louis has a world-class zoo, and it's free. We spent the entire day there, walking animal sanctuary to animal sanctuary. We held hands. We drew stares, but we didn't care. We were young and in love and declaring it.

It was August and hot and we were exhausted when we finished. We went directly to the shower, washed each other, ordered salads and a bottle of wine (there was no ID check over room service), and spent the evening on the couch together. I laid behind him. We were both shirtless. I loved his chest hair and trail, so I played with both throughout the evening as we watched the Cardinals on TV.

I also loved his dick. So, I started playing with it, too. We were 18, and he was soon hard as a rock. I started to jerk him.

"Fuck me while you do that."

We were still on our sides. I spit in my hand, smothered my dick, and slipped easily inside him.

"Don't move. Let's just stay like this for awhile."

I did as I was told. We lay still, my dick inside him, and his dick in my hand. He started clenching and unclenching his ass around my dick. This was a new one, but it was working, fast.

"You keep that up, and I am going to come."

"That's the goal."

I lay still as he continued to work my dick with his ass. I started squeezing his dick, not jerking it, hoping to mirror the sensation I was experiencing. My body broke into a cool sweat as my orgasm approached. I licked his neck and then bit his shoulder as I came. His dick pulsed in my hand as he came. When his dick was too sensitive to touch, he raised my hand to his mouth and sucked his cum off my fingers. I pulled out of him and adjusted my body so I could press my mouth to his, tasting his cum as I kissed him deeply. We kissed until we were both hard again. He broke the kiss, stood up, and took my right hand.

"Let's go to bed."

We climbed into bed and lay face to face. We kissed softly. We ran our hands over each other.

"Roll over."

I did. He wrapped his arms around me and pulled me into a tight embrace. His hair was soft against my back.

"I'm going to miss you."

"I'm going to miss you more."

"I wish we could stay like this forever."

I waited, then I needled him, "I thought you were not going to be my boyfriend."

He chuckled, "Shut up, dork." He kissed the back of my neck. I pushed my ass against him, signaling what I wanted. He rolled me onto my back, and I parted my legs for him. We made slow and steady love. He kissed me as he came. I held him inside me. He collapsed onto me, then rolled off on his side. I pulled the covers up around us and put my face to his. We fell asleep kissing, as had become our custom.

Part Eight

We slept late into Sunday, our last day together before I headed to Carleton and he headed to Loyola of New Orleans, over a thousand miles away. I woke first and just watched him sleep.

I was maudlin, knowing that whatever the last seven weeks had been was going to end, sooner than later. We could pretend otherwise, but I was a realist. We were teenagers, would be separated by over a thousand miles, and would have neither the money nor the means to visit each other. I saw in my mind how it would play out. We would write each other letters, we would talk on the phone each Sunday, and we would see each other when we were home for Fall Homecoming. If we fought hard, and I mean hard, then we would maintain that pattern through the rest of the Fall semester, and we would spend the Christmas break together. But, the Spring semester would be long, and we would get distracted by new friends and experiences. Instead of spending Spring break together, we would spend it apart with new friends. The letters would slow to a trickle and then stop. So would the calls. There would be no emotional rupture. We would just drift away from each other, until we were too far apart to find out way back.

When you are 18 and in love, it is easy to pretend it will last forever, and that you cannot live without the other person. I knew it would not last forever. I also knew I would and could live without Teddy. I just did not want to.

That is what I was thinking when Teddy awoke and smiled at me. I forced a smile back.

"Are you crying?"

"Just a little."

"Why?"

"Because the space shuttle blew up last January, and I miss that teacher," I replied, obviously sarcastically. "Why do you think I'm crying?"

He pulled me tight. "We'll be alright."

"I doubt it."

"I don't."

I did, but there was no point in sharing how I saw it all playing out. There was no reason to make it worse than it was. But, I was pretty convinced of my prescience.

We did not have sex that Sunday morning. Instead, we held each other and kissed and talked and kissed and talked until it was time to check out and accept our separation. We were quiet on the drive back home. I held his hand as he drove. Every once in awhile, he squeezed my hand. I always squeezed back.

The closer we got to my house, the slower he drove. I started to cry, and he did, too. By the time he pulled into my driveway, I was sobbing. He pulled me to him. I buried my head in his neck and chest.

"I love you, dork."

"I love you, too, Teddy. A lot."

Neither of us said another word. We just held each other, crying softly and wanting this salient moment to last as long as we could prolong it. Finally, I pulled back, and he put his lips to mine. We kissed long and deep. When we broke, my parents were on the porch, a lifetime of suspicions confirmed.

"You better go inside. We can't spend the rest of our lives in this car."

I got out of the car, grabbed my bag, and walk around to his door. He cranked his window down.

"Do me a favor at Carleton, Kevin."

"Anything," I offered, almost as a plea.

"Don't be the biggest dork on campus."

He grinned at me. I grinned back. He was beautiful in that moment, sad, but smiling, weak, yet strong.

He slipped the car into reverse, and backed out of the driveway. I watched him go, until his car disappeared around the corner. Crying, I was surprised to feel my dad's hand on my shoulder.

"You'll be alright."

I knew he was wrong. But, I did not say so. Instead, I just turned into his embrace, which was warm and genuine and knowing and loving.

I turned out to be spot on in my prescience. Homecoming weekend was awesome. Since my parents knew about us, we spent most of the weekend in my room. We fucked with a hunger and urgency that only separation could create. We cried when we boarded our planes in opposite directions.

Christmas break was also awesome, but the hunger and urgency of Homecoming weekend was gone. We spent the break together, and we fucked a lot. But, the fire was not as hot. We were not going through the motions, but something was definitely different. We were starting to drift, although neither of us acknowledged it.

As I predicted to myself, we did not see each other over Spring break. Teddy went to Lake Havasu with friends from his fraternity. I stayed in Northfield, working to pay my room and board.

About a month before the end of our freshman year, Teddy told me he was going to spend the summer in New Orleans. I was not surprised. Our hometown was too small for him. I knew it could not hold him long. He was too big.

I spent that summer at home. It was the last time I did. After a year away, I realized our small town was too small to hold me, too. I was too smart. And, with Teddy away, there was not enough to bind me to it.

Teddy and I fell out of contact that summer (there was no such thing as Facebook, texts, Twitter, or Snapchat, there were only letters and landline telephones). He transferred to Rice, because it was more of a science school, and he had immersed himself in Chemistry.

He graduated from Rice and stayed in Houston. I graduated from Carleton and went to the University of Chicago for law school.

He did not show for our five year high school reunion. I went only because I thought he might be there. I left as soon as I realized he wouldn't.

I stayed in Chicago to practice law, raised money for a Senate campaign in 2004, and - in 2012 - was rewarded by the Senator - who was now President - with a federal judgeship. My professional life was awesome, but my personal life was neglected. I barely scratched the surface of those I dated as I lived my life.

As I lived my life, I heard variously from friends about Teddy (I had occasionally trolled for him through Google, LinkedIn, and Facebook, but little turned up). In one report, I heard he married when we were about 30. In another, I heard he had invented something or another, had sold the patent, and had retired with ongoing royalty money that was more than sufficient for him and his family. In the last report, I heard he, his wife, and his four sons (two sets of identical twins born four years apart) now lived on the southern coast of Spain. I also heard he was expected at our 30th reunion, as it coincided with a trip to visit his ailing parents. I had not planned to attend, but I changed my mind as soon as I heard he might.

* * * * *

I was nervous as hell the day of the reunion. We were having a garden party, so it was going to be hot. I could not figure out what to wear to see the lost love of my life for the first time in nearly 30 years. I had loved and lost more than once in those 3 decades, but I never felt the love I had felt for Teddy. First loves are like that, especially teenaged first loves. They expand in our memories. They do not recede.

Frustrated at my indecision, I picked out a pair of cream linen slacks, a white cotton shirt, and a green linen blazer. They were all new. I had spent the prior 90 days trying to rid myself of every vestige of being 48 years old. Once I decided to go to the reunion, I hired a personal trainer that I visited every other day, resumed running on my non-training days, ordered all meals through Evolve, and cut out all alcohol. By the day of the reunion, my stomach was flat, my chest and arms were defined, and my waist was narrow.

I arrived right on time. I said hello to the few people I recognized, and then I scanned the party for Teddy. Not seeing him, I waited in line at the bar for what I assumed would be a perfectly awful plastic glass of cheap red wine. As I waited, I felt a familiar hand on my shoulder.

"Hey, dork."

I turned around to look into Teddy's incandescent blue eyes for the first time since Christmas, 1986. He smiled that same smile. Before I got lost in it, I smiled back. He pulled me into a deep embrace that betrayed 30 years of neglect. Neither of us could pull away. I melted into him, utterly and completely relaxed and lost. He dug his hands into my back and let out a long, forlorn sigh. I have no idea how long we stayed like that, but the embrace had to hint to our classmates that they did not know all there was to know about Teddy and me.

When we parted, he complimented me. "You look great, dork. Really really great." He stepped back and looked me up and down. His eyes were glistening with tears.

I looked at him through my own wet eyes and smiled. "You look bald, Teddy. Really really bald." I was not surprised. Chest hair on a teenager often leads to early onset baldness.

He laughed and added, "And fat."

"I wouldn't say that."

"Well, I certainly have some extra 'retired, married' weight on me that you don't."

"Well, I am neither retired nor married. And, to be perfectly honest, I have lived on the edge of starvation for the last 90 days because I thought I might run into you here. And, I wanted to look like you remembered."

He smiled deeply at me again. It was a knowing, intimate, but regretful smile.

"You look exactly like I remember."

"You look better."

"Insincerity does not suit you, dork."

We smiled and stared at each other too long. He broke the stare.

"Let's get a drink and go for a walk," he suggested.

We did. Neither of us spoke. When we were far enough away, he took my hand in his. He squeezed. I squeezed back. Love poured out in those squeezes.

"Are you with anyone?"

"No."

"Why not?"

"I was waiting for you."

He looked at me quizzically. I smiled.

"I'm kidding. I dunno, I just have not found someone special enough to make me forget someone so special."

"That's too bad. You would make someone really happy. You made me really, really happy."

"Not happy enough."

"That's not fair. We were teenagers. We were miles away from each other. It was a different time. We never would have lasted."

"We could have tried."

"You're right. We could have."

"I wanted to."

He did not respond. He walked a little ahead of me and turned around.

"I wanted to, too. I just didn't know how. . . . Do you ever wonder what life would have been like if we had?"

He smiled a rueful smile. His eyes were glistening again.

"I do, all the time," I said.

"Me, too," he admitted.

We walked on, silently. We had said all there was to say. We had said almost nothing at all.

Part Nine

Although Teddy and I exchanged contact information, I thought it was a mere formality. We had said all there was to say. Our paths, once entwined, had diverged dramatically, his toward what he expected of himself, and mine toward what I wanted for myself.

About a year after our 30th reunion, I heard that Teddy's wife, Melissa, had died of breast cancer. It was hopeless by the time they caught it. I thought of reaching out to Teddy, but I feared it would appear hollow. Or predatory. I still regret letting my fear get the best of me. Fear is almost always wrong.

About nine months after Melissa's death, I received a surprising email. "Have you ever been to Spain?"

I was not sure if I should respond. I was not sure how to respond. "No" seemed honest, but curt. "No, but I would like to," seemed honest but needy. "Why do you ask?" seemed opaque and disingenuous. So, I did not respond. I typed many responses, but I did not send any of them.

A few days later, I received another email, forwarding the prior one. "This email is intended for Kevin Michaels. If this is not the correct email address for Kevin, then please let me know. Thank you." I had to respond.

"This is the correct email address. I have tried to respond, but I was not sure how to/what to say. I am sorry."

Quickly, I received a reply. "It's a simple question. Have you ever been to Spain?"

Later that evening, I replied. "No, I have not ever been to Spain. And, I am sorry about Melissa. I wanted to reach out, but I was not sure how to/what to say. I am sorry."

I did not realize my email had almost mirrored my earlier one, but Teddy did not miss it. "When did you become so diffident? And, are you just cutting and pasting? Stop apologizing. There is nothing to apologize for. Melissa's death was sad, but we had a good marriage, the best part of which is our four boys. I miss her every day, but I need to let go of the past and move forward, before I am too old and it's too late."

I did not respond.

The next day, I received a follow up. "You should come to Spain."

"When?"

"As soon as possible."

"Why?"

"Because I said so, dork. Quit being opaque."

As a federal judge, my schedule booked up months in advance. The following Monday, I asked my Assistant when I could next take a two week break from the bench. She laughed.

"Your next two week block is in 2020, two years from now."

I emailed Teddy. "My schedule is a wreck. I do not have a two week block for 18 months or so."

I received a response almost immediately. He had cut and pasted it from an earlier email. "I need to let go of the past and move forward, before I am too old and it is too late."

Teddy's email vexed me. I was the past. The distant past, in fact. I decided to call him on it.

"I am the past, so I am not sure what this is all about."

I received a response almost immediately again. "You have never been the past. Whether you knew it or not, you were always with me."

I took control of my own calendar. I had a two week civil trial set in six weeks. It was almost certainly going to settle, as 98% of all civil cases do. And, this was a dud civil case, of interest to no one other than maybe the parties involved. It certainly no longer interested me. I exercised my Article III powers, ordered the case to mediation, and vacated the trial date until after any mediation.

With two weeks suddenly free, I booked a flight to Madrid and emailed Teddy. "I cleared two weeks in August. I land in Madrid at 3 p.m. on the 11th. I leave at 1 p.m. on the 25th. I have no plans in between."

Teddy's reply did not come for almost a day. "You will miss the boys, as they will be in the states the entire month of August with Melissa's family."

Teddy's email again vexed me. I had expected something a little more effusive. Or excited. I decided to let it sit, unanswered.

I heard nothing for weeks. The silence made me wonder if I had not jumped the gun in making reservations. Then, about a week before I was supposed to board a plane that I thought may actually travel back in time, I received the following:

"Hey, dork. I am excited to see you. We have two weeks to ourselves. I hope we can turn back the clock. If not, then I hope we have a future of friendship and warm memories. Still lots of love, Teddy."

My vexation was resolved. I was traveling toward a second chance, 32 years after the first chance expectedly failed. I was both giddy and terrified.

Teddy met my flight. He greeted me briefly and warmly.

"Welcome to Spain, dork."

"Glad to be here."

"You need anything? We have a long drive ahead of us."

Teddy's house was on the outskirts of Malaga, more than 5 hours away by car. We grabbed waters and my bags and drove off. Teddy filled the hours by telling me about his four boys, now motherless at 16 and 12 (he had two sets of identical twins, the first set 2 years after marrying Melissa and the second set 4 years later). And, about the death of Melissa, which had obviously been devastating to their family. Melissa had been the tie that bound, and the AAtreyu boys had foundered in her absence.

As we drove, I noticed that Teddy was much leaner and much more muscled than he had been at the 30th reunion. Grief had apparently suppressed his appetite, and the gym had been an apparent outlet for the same grief.

"I am very sorry about Melissa."

"Me, too. But, better to have loved and lost than never to have loved, right? At least that is what a dorky kid told me a long time ago when things were coming undone."

I looked at Teddy. He was smiling at me. Sooner than I expected to be, I was again lost in him. He had remembered our last phone call, when it had all come undone.

A train, two planes, and an automobile behind me, I was beat when we got to his modest, beautiful house. In fact, I had slept the last hour or so of the drive.

I knew little Spanish, but I knew the sign out front meant the house was for sale.

"You moving?"

"Yes, too many old memories in this house. And, not enough room for new ones." I did not ask to where, but I should have.

Once we unloaded the car, Teddy showed me to my room, and left me to shower and join him for what I thought was a late dinner but which, for Spain, was not late at all. I never made it to dinner. After my shower, I laid down on the bed to rest my eyes. I woke up 12 hours later, my clothes removed (except my boxers), my bags unpacked, and the covers pulled to my chin. I had slept through our first night together, including apparently through being stripped and tucked in.

When I wandered into the kitchen, Teddy was busy making breakfast. He was wearing only gym shorts. He was still bald. His chest hair was clippered, as were his pits, his arm hair, his leg hair, and his path to paradise. His muscles were long and sinewy, and the manscaping only enhanced the definition. He cut quite an image. When he looked at me with his blue eyes and smiled, the image took my breath away.

"Good morning, dork. I was afraid you would sleep the trip away."

"Good morning. Thank you for taking care of me last night."

"I want to take care of you every night."

I paused. I was not sure where he was coming from, but this seemed like too much too fast for me. So, I balked.

"Teddy, what is this?"

"Look, dork, I let you go once. I do not want to do it again. I have thought of you and us every day since the reunion, always wondering what might have been. I think we have a second chance to find out. We missed the first chance. I do not want to miss this one."

"Are you sure you're not just lonely or still dealing with the grief of Melissa?"

"I have been lonely my whole life. Melissa was a great wife, but I have been lonely for you since there was no more you. I wondered for a long time why I did not reconnect with you, and the reunion made me realize why. I would not have been able to bear it, whether it was the thought of what we missed, or the thought of you finding what we lost with someone else. So, I stayed away. After the reunion, I was terribly sad. Palpably so. Melissa knew something was wrong, and she would not let it go. She goaded me into telling her what. So, I told her about you. Everything. We were trying to figure out our future, if we had one, when she got diagnosed. Then, there was nothing to figure out, so we put everything on hold. I have been on hold for two years. I do not want to be on hold any more."

I sat silent and still and tried to take it all in. Teddy walked over to me, took my hand in his, and said "You can't be surprised. You dropped everything and flew all the way to Spain to find out, didn't you?"

With that, he leaned down and kissed me. As we kissed, I hurtled back in time. As our tongues touched, I was 18, it was the summer of 1986 again, we did not have a care in the world, and our future was full of nothing but promise. As I rose to meet the kiss, Teddy clamped his arms around me. I clamped my arms around him. Our bodies were pressed hard against each other. His hands went to my head, pressing me to him and trying to deepen the kiss. My hands went to his back, and I pressed his chest into mine as hard as I could. I do not know how long that kiss lasted, but 32 years disappeared into it.

When we finally broke the kiss, Teddy turned off the burners and abandoned the breakfast. I followed him to his room. We kissed again, just as long and as intently as before. These were forgiving kisses, forgetting kisses, promising kisses.

Teddy tugged my shirt over my head and then pressed his bare chest to mine. My skin tingled with familiarity and newness. I hooked my arms under his and buried my face in his chest. He pulled me as tight as he could. I breathed him in.

I could feel Teddy's hard dick against my stomach. I easily lowered his gym shorts.

"Take yours off, too."

I did.

"I have not had sex since I told Melissa about us. And, I have not had sex with another man since you."

I was unsure of the need to share that information, and I could not say the same. I had had a lot of sex recently, and all my sex since him was with other men.

"Good to know, I guess."

"I mean, I doubt I will last long." He was right, as he came almost as soon as I grabbed his dick, before we even got into bed.

"I'm sorry. So, so sorry."

"Don't worry about it. We have a lot of time together."

I pulled him down on top of me on the bed, and he kissed me again. This was our third kiss of the morning, and I am certain that - with the other two - it was one of the top three kisses of all time. They felt like traveling at the speed of light. They felt like not moving at all.

Teddy finally pulled his lips from mine and started kissing my face. He kissed my neck and my chest. He kissed my arms and my armpits. He kissed my stomach and my abdomen. He kissed my pelvis and where my legs meet my groin. He kissed and licked my balls. He took me in his mouth. I came just as fast as he had, filling his mouth before he could even start working me. He pulled off and spit.

"Sorry about that," I said, offering the second sex apology of the morning.

"I have not done this for a long time. I did not mean to spit. I was just caught off guard."

I pulled him back to me, and he flopped down on his left side next to me. I turned to him, and he pressed his lips gently to mine. I put my hand in the middle of his chest and felt his heart beat. He put his hand to my cheek.

"I have missed you so much, dork," he offered. "I need you to know that I thought about you all the time. You were always with me."

"I never stopped loving you," I responded. "You were always with me."

We kissed again. As we did, I started to cry, and so did he. Teddy licked my tears off my cheeks and then kissed them into my mouth. We stared into each other's eyes for what seemed like forever. We said everything we had to say without saying anything at all. Our story had re-started. What was lost was found.

The next two weeks sped by. We took languid walks and had furtive sex. We sat quietly and fucked loudly. My last night in Spain, we made excruciating love. We were on the living room floor. I was on my back, my legs and arms wrapped around him. Teddy's arms were hooked under mine and wrapped around my shoulders. Everything about us was needy. I was at his mercy. The vulnerability was intoxicating and liberating and frightening and consuming.

Teddy slowly delivered himself to me, never letting his lips leave my lips or his chest leave my chest. For the first time during the visit, he was not fucking me. He was making love to me.

I was wide open to him. He could not go too slow or too deep. I rose to meet him, keeping my lips to his lips and my chest to his chest.

"I love you so much, Kevin."

"I love you, too, Teddy."

The deliberate pace of our lovemaking did not mask the passion that was driving it. I was disappearing into Teddy, and he was disappearing into me.

Teddy continued his deliberate pace. Every time he got close, he backed off. Each time the delay was more difficult to bear. I was needy for him to fill me.

"I need you to fuck me."

"I am fucking you."

"No, I need to you fuck me."

Teddy smiled at me and picked up his pace. As he did, I continued to meet him, and we both started to sweat. Our kisses turned sloppy and urgent. I sucked Teddy's tongue as he pounded into me. I could not get him in deep enough, even using my hands and feet as leverage.

"Arch your back."

When he did, he penetrated me as deeply as he could. I arched my neck and back as I came. Teddy's orgasm followed a short time later, filling me. Before I knew it, I was coming again, and I spilled another load between us. Teddy kept fucking me. Just when I thought I could not take another stroke, he came again, crying out as he did.
After he had filled me for the second time, Teddy collapsed onto me, mixing our sweat with my cum. I grabbed his face, and he grabbed mine. I looked deeply into his eyes, and I knew him as I had that summer 32 years before.

"I don't want you to leave."

"I have to. My job is in Chicago waiting for me."

"Then I am coming with you."

"Seriously?"

"Why do you think I put the house on the market? And, why do you think I already moved my boys to the states?"

"That seems presumptuous. How did you know this would work?"

"We're us. We always have been. And, I saw it in your eyes at the reunion. And, I felt it in your touch when I held your hand."

He was right. Our life affair had re-started at the reunion. I just had not known it.

I flew home the next day full of love and hope. Past is prologue. Our future was ours.

Teddy was to follow six weeks later, picking up his boys on the way. In the meantime, I sold my Gold Coast condominium (it was barely large enough for me, much less me and five more men) and bought a four bedroom bungalow in Evanston. I had been pretty much alone for 32 years. I soon no longer would be. My solitary life was yielding to the past, and my past was my future.

Part Ten

The six weeks after my return from Spain were a whirlwind, and I got vertiginous in it. Normally hyper-rational and deliberate, I had thoughtlessly made monumental life decisions on the fly and based on nothing other than craven emotion. My friends had tried to reign me in, to slow me down, to talk even a scintilla of sense into me, but I was not to be deterred. I was like a bull that had seen red. I charged.

The day before Teddy and his boys were to arrive, the whirlwind stopped spinning, I got my bearings back, and I freaked out. I was gripped by fear bordering on panic. Based on a two week vacation, I had agreed for all intents and purposes to marry an ostensibly straight man and help him raise his four teen-aged boys, who likely were still reeling emotionally from the tragic death of their mother and who almost certainly were going to be rocked, if not wrecked, by the idea of their father loving and fucking another man. Yes, there was some history behind those two weeks, but that history was ancient. Teddy did not really know me anymore, I did not really know him anymore, and I certainly did not know Matthew and Mark (the 16 year old set of twins) or Kurt and Kyle (the 12 year old set). I also knew nothing about parenting, much less about parenting teenaged boys. My own parents had been tragic parenting failures. My only experience as a caregiver had been with a rescue cat, and I had abandoned him to my best friend, Thom. All three of us were happier with Elmer in Thom's care. I'd have killed him.

I was in Evanston alone, so my support structure was not even proximate. They were all down in the city I had hastily abandoned on a lark.

Frozen to inaction, I called Thom. He answered after the first ring. He knew me better than I knew myself.

"Scared shitless aren't you?"

"Yes, how did you know?"

"Because, tomorrow, the dream becomes reality, and shit gets real."

"How could I have been so naive? I don't know him, he doesn't know me, and I don't know his kids at all. I have never even met them, and they are moving in here tomorrow. I don't even know if they know why they are moving to the Chicago suburbs."

"Honey, you got caught up in the fairy tale. We all want to live happily ever after. But, you know what my mother used to say, 'want in one hand and shit in the other and see which fills up first.'"

"Your mother had a wonderful way with words."

"You know it."

"Tell me it will be okay."

"It will be okay."

"Tell me again, and, this time, mean it."

"You know I can't do that. You are too smart for that. It very well may not be okay. But, I can tell you that I hope it is. I hope your dreams come true. I hope it's the fucking gay Brady Bunch for you and this guy I have never met. But, if it isn't, I'll be here to help you piece your shattered life back together."

"Is it going to be awful?"

"I don't know if it will be awful. But, it will be hard. Really, really hard. Like harder than anything you have ever done. But, I admire you for trying to do it."

"Thanks."

"Just keep a level head and keep getting back up again. You know, it's not how many times you get knocked down, it's how many times you get back up."

"From your mother?"

"Nope. I am not sure where I got that. Probably off one of those horrible inspirational posters with kittens or dogs preaching 'faith isn't faith until it's all you're holding onto'."

"Thanks, Thom."

"You betcha, Kevo. Good luck tomorrow. And, call every time you need to."

"I will."

I should have hung up, but I could not. We just listened to each other breathe. We did this a lot. It was comforting. It was like holding each other in the modern, wireless world. I don't know how long we sat like that, but Thom broke the trance at just the right time, just as I was starting to freak again.

"Listen, dude, you are the smartest and the strongest guy I know. If anyone can do this, you can. Remember to hold on tight, but not so tight you choke off the oxygen."

"I love you, Thom."

"I love you, too, brother. Now, go take a Xanax."

We hung up. I felt reinforced, but still very fragile. As urged, I took a Xanax. And drank a bottle of wine on my screened porch.

When I woke up, it was morning. Teddy and his boys were driving in and due to arrive that evening. I frantically put the finishing touches on the three bedrooms that were not mine, one for Matthew and Mark, one for Kurt and Kyle, and one for Teddy, as I was not sure what he had told his boys or what the arrangements would or should be as they got settled. The house had two masters, and I set each of them up for the twin sets. If they were going to have to share rooms, they at least needed to be spacious with their own bathrooms.

By the time they pulled up outside, I was a bundle of jangled, exposed nerves. I had also dropped another Xanax and was well into a bottle of wine.

As they trudged up the walk, they looked beat or beaten. I could not decoct which.

I opened the door before they rang or knocked. No one spoke, other than Teddy, who unaffectionately said "hello." We stood awkwardly and silently in the foyer, like boxers trying to get the feel of the fight. Finally, Teddy asked me to show them to their rooms. I did. Matthew and Mark immediately went into theirs and closed the door behind them. Kurt and Kyle did the same. Then, Teddy did as well. I was alone on the landing in a house full of strange men. I felt like an innkeeper. Or a butler. I went downstairs and finished off the bottle of red and made dinner. When no one came downstairs, I went up and knocked on Teddy's door. When he opened, his expression of defeat floored me. I grabbed him and held him. He sank into me.

"That bad?" I knew from our calls that Teddy planned to spend the drive from D.C. to Chicago talking his boys through the changes that were coming.

"Worse."

"I made dinner."

"I doubt there will be any dinner tonight, at least for the boys."

"How bad was it?"

"It was to be expected, I guess. I got so caught up in you, I forgot about them. I'm their father. I cannot forget about them, and I feel like shit for having done so. And, I was utterly and completely naive to think they would just accept all this upheaval on the heels of their mother's death. They did not, and they called me out on it. I think I got ahead of myself on this one. I certainly got ahead of them."

"I know what you mean. I had a massive panic attack yesterday and another one today. We don't know each other. Not really. And, I don't know your boys at all. And, they certainly do not know me. Yet, here we all are, 6 strangers thrown together in a strange house."

"We do know each other. At least how it matters. But, we are going to have to quell that for awhile. I got interrogated on the drive. 'So, you're gay now? Were you always gay? Was your marriage to mom just a big lie? Did mom know? Who is this guy? Did he trick you? Is he supposed to take our mom's place? How could you move on so fast?' It was awful."

"We need to give them time. We need to give us time."

Teddy took my hand. "I'm not worried about us. I'm really not. We'll bump around a bit, hit a few snags, figure out how to fit together, but we'll be fine." He paused. "Actually, we'll be better than fine. We were meant to be, and we'll be great. But, I'm not so sure about the boys."

Teddy followed me downstairs. We ate together and talked. It may have been the Xanax and the wine, but it felt comfortable, familiar, old. Like it was like it was supposed to be. When we finished, we took plates up to the boys and sat them outside their bedroom doors. I went into my bedroom while Teddy knocked and tried to persuade them through their doors to eat.

When Teddy went into his room, I was sitting on his bed.

"How did you get in here?"

"Through the bathroom. It's a jack and jill. It connects our rooms. The boys have the masters. I claimed these two rooms for the access. I thought it would be easier on them if you did not just move into my room."

Teddy smiled at me. Unless his boys were dumb, they'd soon figure out why they got the master suites. In the meantime, Teddy used the access to join me that night after he had tried and failed to talk to his boys out of their rooms. We tried to be quiet, but we were not. We tried to resolve all of our doubts with the sureness and certainty of our love-making. We kissed each other and we sucked each other and we fucked each other until we were exhausted. We fell asleep naked and wrapped up in each other, the doors to our rooms locked so we would not be discovered. As I fell asleep, I knew Teddy was right. He and I would be great. It was the boys we had to fret over.

Teddy's boys were not dumb. I did not expect them to be, but they resolved even the hint of a doubt the following morning (a Sunday) at breakfast. They grilled me and their father. A former lawyer, I held my own. But, only barely. Their father got ransacked. In the end, the boys made clear they were not happy about Teddy and me, they were not happy about what "we" were doing, they were not happy about Teddy "moving on" from their mother, and they were not happy to be in Evanston and had no plans to stay, if they could help it. They had already talked to their grandparents about staying with them in D.C., and they were urging that solution on us. The confrontation had been seething. They were going to be tough nuts to crack, and I had no analogous experience from which to draw.

I noted as they confronted us how disparate the boys were. Matthew was older than Mark by 2 minutes or so, but it could easily have been two years. He bore all the traits of the oldest child. He was the alpha, and he spoke for the group. He was confident and certain and enraged, although he never raised his voice. He hissed beneath his father's blue eyes (he and Mark

94

looked almost exactly like their father had when I had met him oh so long ago).

Mark was similar to Matthew only in appearance. In personality, he was far more reserved and taciturn. It was clear he deferred to Matthew. He had said very little that morning, expressing himself mostly through his glare and occasional grimaces.

Kurt and Kyle looked and acted almost the same. In appearance, they favored their mother, which was too bad for them. They were okay looking, but their older brothers were striking. In action, they were ebullient. They smiled broadly and easily, almost constantly. They were going to be easier, at least I thought they were. But, they were diffident, and they deferred to Matthew.

Teddy was a good father, I could tell. Although he got ransacked by his boys, he did not get angry or reactive. He listened more than he spoke. He never got defensive. I took my cue from him, although I said very little except in response to direct questions.

After the confrontation, the boys retreated to their rooms, and Teddy and I went out onto the screened porch. Teddy went first.

"We need to formulate a plan and answer their questions."

"I agree," I said, as I started taking notes. I am a visual person and a chronic note-taker.

Teddy and I talked all day. By dinner, we had five talking points to share with the boys. Teddy laid them out over dinner, which he had made mandatory.

"I listened to the four of you this morning. I did. I really listened. Now, I want you to listen to me. To really listen. First, I know this is tough on you. I really do. I understand your reaction, and I appreciate it. I need you to understand that I understand.

"Second, you will respect me and you will respect Kevin. I am your parent, and I will be making the parenting decisions. But, Kevin will have input, and you will treat him at all times with respect. You do not have to love him, although I think you will, or even like him, which I am sure you will. But, you do have to respect him.

"Third, it is time for the pouting and the insolence to end. It is not going to have the hoped for effect. We are not going back to Spain. We are not going somewhere else. You are not going to D.C. You are staying here, with me. You can choose to like it, or you can choose to hate it. It's your choice. I hope you choose to like it, as it will make all of our lives better. But, whether you choose to like it or hate it, it is time for you stop acting like the brats you are not.

"Fourth, you will have input into all aspects of living in this house. But, the final decisions will be mine and Kevin's. We will talk them through with you before they are made. But, once they are made, they are made, and you need to accept them.

"Finally, I love you unconditionally. I always have and I always will. I would like the same in return, and I have not been getting that recently from any of you."

Teddy's eyes glistened as he finished. "After dinner, I want all four of you to go to your rooms, to sit down, and to think long and hard about how lucky you are. You have a great father. You had a great mother, which is a lot more than a lot of kids can say. You have great brothers. You have money, you have stuff, you live needless lives. And, the new life that you are so pissed off about is in a great home in a great suburb of a great city in a great country. Yes, I am asking you to make adjustments. But, that's life. We always have to adjust. But, through it all, we are and always will be us. The rest is just window dressing."

All four boys were crying by the time Teddy finished. So was I. We ate in silence. When dinner was over, the boys all did as they had been told. Teddy told me to go to bed, he would clean the kitchen. He wanted to be alone to think.

I was asleep by the time Teddy slid in next to me.

"I think that went well. I think you got through to them."

"We'll see."

"You seem circumspect."

"They're teenaged boys. They think they know everything. And, they think I don't know anything. So, we'll see."

I rolled into him. As we had the night before, we kissed and sucked and fucked until we were spent. It was lazy, as there was for the first time in our lives together no clock ticking. After, I lay with my head on his shoulder and my hand in his chest hair.

"What did you tell them when they asked if you were gay?"

"The truth."

"What's that?"

"That I fell in love with you when I was in high school, that we drifted apart when we were in college, that I dated a lot of girls through my 20s, that I never thought I was the marrying kind until I met their mother, that I loved her very much through every minute of our marriage and never betrayed her, that her death almost killed me, and that I reconnected with you after she died and found hope where I thought there was none. And, that I did not know what that made me, and I saw no need to try to label it."

I stewed on his answer for a bit. "What did they say?"

"Matthew scoffed 'That's total bullshit. You're at least bi, if not a total fag.'"

I started to laugh. Teddy laughed, too.

When I stopped laughing, I laid bare the elephant in the room.

"They're going to be tougher than I thought."

"Yep."

Part Eleven

Teddy was right. They were a lot tougher than I thought. At least Matthew and Mark were. Their tears of that Sunday dinner notwithstanding, Matthew treated me with barely respectful contempt thereafter. Mark took his lead from his twin.

They treated their father slightly better. But only slightly. I feared they were headed toward rupture.

Kurt and Kyle were stuck in the middle. They wanted and needed their father, but they also wanted and needed their older brothers, and they did not want to move toward one and alienate the other. They were not adroit enough to straddle the two camps.

We had kept the boys out of school for the Fall semester, thinking it would help them adjust to their new lives not to start at a new school mid-semester. That was probably a mistake, as it meant the five of them were circling each other all day. Their January return to school could not come soon enough.

With their input, we had settled on a private Evanston school for their return. We all thought it would be easier for them to transition into a smaller, private school than into a large, public one. We also thought the small, private school would be more understanding of their alternative, but not unique, living situation. It was going to be expensive (about $15,000 per year per child), but Teddy did not seem concerned about the price.

As the holidays approached, the house was a tinder box. Matthew and so Mark, too, were sullen and surly. Kyle and Kurt were pensive and diffident. Teddy was helpless, having exhausted all options he and our counselor could think of to bring Matthew and Mark around. And, I lurked in the shadows of my own home, especially where the boys were concerned. I felt like I was walking on melting ice. At least I had my chambers and the gym to retreat to.

The only place in the entire house that was loose and free was the bed Teddy and I shared nightly. We were like teenagers again, kissing and sucking and fucking with reckless abandon. Teddy had decided that, since Matthew and Mark (we called them "M&M" or, when we wanted to piss them off, the "candy boys") seemed entrenched in their disdain, there was no reason to shelter them from what was going on in the house. So, Teddy stopped pretending to have his own room, and moved into mine. And, he stopped trying to shield them from what happened in our room. We kept our door closed, but we no longer came quietly or tried to stifle our pleasure.

Outside of M&M, Teddy and I were slowly, surely fitting together. As unlikely as it seemed after 32 years, we still fit hand in glove. He slipped into my life like one would slip into a comfortable, familiar sweater. My friends liked Teddy very much, at times, it seemed, more than they liked me. And, Teddy seemed settled in his new life, however he labeled or did not label it.

But, something had to give in the house. The atmosphere was just not healthy, especially for Kurt and Kyle. They were being pulled thin, like carnival taffy. We had to act before they broke.

The solution came from Matthew over a mid-December dinner.

"Dad, Mark and I have been talking, and we don't want to go to the school you picked."

"We picked," Teddy corrected, kindly.

"Whatever. You picked. We picked. He picked. We all picked. It doesn't matter. We don't want to go there."

"Well, the public school is certainly good and less expensive, but you are likely to face more problems there."

"We do not want to go there, either."

Teddy stopped eating and focused on Matthew.

"We want to go away. To a boarding school. We don't want to live with you and him."

"Use Kevin's name, please."

"Fine. We don't want to live with you and Kevin." He had hit my name hard, obviously to convey contempt for having to use it.

I picked up my plate and left the table. I was not angry at the slight. I was conflicted. I selfishly loved Matthew's solution, but it seemed permanent, and I did not want to be the reason Teddy and his oldest boys cleaved in two. I finished my dinner on the screened porch. Kurt and Kyle joined me as I did, I later found out at their father's direction.

To say I got along better with Kurt and Kyle than I did with M&M was an understatement. I got along better with anyone and everyone better than I got along with M&M. With my therapist, I posited that I should not really blame them after all the tumult they had been through, that they may see my presence as an act of betrayal against their martyred mother, that they were teenaged boys wrought with hormones and change and not sure how to deal with that toxic combination, all sorts of solid, rational explanations for the cold war that gripped our house. But, at my core, I thought they were just insufferable little dicks, and I could not believe how far off they were from their father. I had never met Melissa, but if they took after her, I am glad I hadn't.

"Do you boys want to go away to school, too?" I asked.

Kyle and Kurt looked stunned by my question and then looked at each other.

Kyle started, "No, sir. We want to stay with our dad."

Looking at me, Kurt added, "And with you."

I could not help myself. I grabbed them both and pulled them in. The tension in the house was palpable, and those three words had cut through it for me. I started to cry. When I did, they collectively squeezed me. I felt ice melting, walls coming down, barricades being breached.

We were holding each other like that when Teddy finished talking to Matthew and Mark and found me on the porch. Without saying a word, Teddy joined the embrace. I did not realize it then, but the symbolism was ripe. The four of us were pulling together, and M&M wanted no part of it.

As was our custom, Teddy and I did not talk through the decision in front of the boys. Instead, we waited until we were in our room for "quiet time."

"Quiet time" Teddy's invention, I think mostly to avoid fracture in the house. At 8:30 p.m. Monday through Thursday, all televisions were off, the downstairs was dark, and all of us were in our respective rooms with doors closed to read, write, work, or, in our case, talk and fuck. The television rule was easy, as none of us had one in our room.

While stripping down, Teddy raised the subject. "What do you think?"

"I don't know what to think, Teddy. Part of me thinks we should send them off tomorrow, but that's just me being selfish. Most of me thinks I should find an apartment and not be the reason the AAtreyu boys break up."

"Are you ready to give up on us?"

"I'm not suggesting that. We can stay together, just under different roofs so there can be some sense of detente."

"That is not going to work. They just made it very clear. They - and I say 'they,' but this is mostly Matthew - want to go away unless you are out of the picture completely. That's their 'deal.'"

Revulsion overwhelmed me. I thought I was going to throw up. Or pass out. They were making Teddy choose between me and them. It had to be an easy choice for him, and it had to be them. He was their father. I was his past.

I looked at Teddy. He immediately read my thoughts.

"Kevin, the decision's easy. They have a list of schools, and we are going to leave tomorrow to visit them. Kurt and Kyle can stay here, if that's okay with you."

"It is. But, are you sure about this?"

"Yes. The situation here is untenable. It has been from the start. If they go away, I am not going to lose my boys. They will just be leaving a little sooner than I expected. But, if they stay, I am definitely going to lose you. And, I am not willing to let that happen."

"Aren't they going to feel like this is some huge betrayal, that you picked me over them?"

"I hope not. I just explained that is not what is happening. I told them I thought they had offered a very adult solution to a very adult problem, and I appreciated their willingness to talk it through with me. They seem enthralled with the idea of boarding school. I think they forced the choice on me only to force me to agree to let them go. I think they know I would have said no otherwise."

I did not sleep that night. I feared I had come between Teddy and his sons, and he would resent me for it, even if he thought he would not. I was the realist who saw things as they were. He was the optimist who saw things as he wanted.

Teddy and Matthew and Mark drove off the next day to visit a half-dozen elite, East coast boarding schools. Kurt, Kyle, and I stayed behind. With no trials scheduled for the following week, I planned to work from home as much as I could, so I could spend time with Kurt and Kyle. And, because I did not trust two 12 year old boys at home alone for a week.

Teddy was buoyant when he reported in on their visits. He said M&M's attitude and demeanor changed as soon as they pulled out of the garage and started their drive east. Their icy approach toward him thawed. They were excited and excitable again.

I assured him that Kurt, Kyle, and I were having a great time as well. With the pall of the "candy boys" lifted, Kurt and Kyle brightened and filled out. They talked and talked and talked. I heard all about their childhood in Spain, the loss of their mother, their August with their grandparents, and their plan to talk their father into letting them take the whole year away from school. According to them, they needed a "gap" year. Kyle asked if I thought their father would say "yes" if they told him they would leave if he didn't. I could tell by the glint in his eye he didn't mean it. But, I decided to play along.

"No, I think he will let you leave, just like he did with the 'candy boys.'"

"He wanted them to leave. They've been such dicks. He'll want us to stay. We're not like them."

"True, but he also knows you want to stay. So, he'll call your bluff and tell you you can leave, knowing you won't."

"You think he's that smart."

"You know him better than I do. What do you think?"

"He's that smart."

Our week was like that. I settled into this alien role of caregiver. And, Kyle and Kurt accepted me in that role. Teddy was going to be shocked when he returned.

When he did, he and the "candy boys" had settled on a school. It was small and elite and expensive at $20,000 per semester per student. I made $189,000 per year as a federal judge. I had some savings, but $80,000 per year for 2.5 years would deplete it rapidly.

During quiet time, I broached the subject. "Can we afford this school?"

"Sure," he said, so cavalierly that my interest was piqued.

"Maybe I shouldn't ask this, but how much money do you have?"

"Enough."

"Enough for what?"

"Enough for anything."

I raised an eyebrow at him.

"Let me put it this way. I don't have to work. You don't have to work. And, the boys will never have to work, if they don't want to. And the boys' children will not have to work, if they don't want to."

"Holy shit. . . . Just from some formula?"

"I was a very commercial formula. Billions have been made from it and will continue to be. As they are, I get my little share and will continue to. But, more than half the money came from Melissa. She had a large trust fund. I inherited it when she died."

I relaxed against my pillow. "I better be getting one helluva Christmas present. Speaking of which, what do you want for Christmas?"

"You already gave me my gift."

"Really . . . . what?"

"Watching you and Kurt and Kyle tonight. It was like watching, I don't know, a father with his two sons maybe. I am not sure what you did while I was gone, but it was the best gift you could ever give me. The four of us are going to be very happy in this house."

Teddy kissed me. "I love you, Kevin."

"I love you, too."

"What do you want for Christmas?"

"I'm easy," I said, as I grabbed his dick. "This."

Our house had turned a corner. The "candy boys" were looking forward to leaving the house, and their impending departure was like the sun peaking out after days and days of cold, grey rain. And, it had freed them from some of their demons. They were not quite friendly, but they were friendlier.

The anticipation liberated us that night. I worked Teddy's dick with my mouth like I had not in a long time, repeatedly bringing him to the edge of orgasm before backing off. When he finally came, it was an enormous load. I took it all and continued to work my "gift" with my mouth and my tongue until he could not take any more.

I straddled Teddy's chest and buried my dick in his mouth. This was his favorite position to suck me, as it gave him the best view of the V that formed my pelvis. And, it allowed me the best leverage to fuck his face. I controlled my own orgasm in this

111

position, and I had no interest in delaying it as I had delayed his. I filled his mouth as soon as I could and then collapsed onto him.

If we had been adults, that probably would have been enough. But, we were not. We were teenagers again. It was 1986, and love was in the air. So, I kissed his face, smelled his armpits, sucked his nipples, and licked his navel before lathering his dick with my spit and riding him recklessly, carelessly, freely. He cried out when he came. His cry released me, and I came without touching myself all over his chest and stomach. When neither of us could take any more, I collapsed onto him again, smearing my cum between our sweaty bodies.

We slept like that, slimy and dirty and then dry and sticky. We were awaked by Kurt and Kyle climbing into our bed the next morning, the first time they had done that since they moved in. Through some clever maneuvering of our thick, down comforter, we were able to hide both our nudity and the remnants of our "quiet time" the prior night, but we were going to have to remember to lock our door going forward. Or, at least, to take showers before going to sleep.

They climbed between us. As Kurt rested his head on his dad's shoulder, Kyle rested his on mine. It felt like a family. As we laid there listening to the house wake up, the sun shone brightly through the shades and into our room. For the first time in a long time.

Part Twelve

As a condition of sending M&M away, their father insisted they attend weekly therapy sessions. They needed it. They had been through a lot. Being teenaged boys is difficult enough without the added tumult of the death of a parent, a repatriation from a leisurely life in Spain, and the introduction of me and a life they never expected from or for their father.

Whether it was the therapy or just being away, M&M seemed to be thriving in New Hampshire, both academically and socially. But, the wall between themselves and their father remained solid. Therapy did not crease it, much less crack it. M&M talked to their brothers regularly, but not often to their father. And never to, or even of, me. The Ks had learned to avoid the topic altogether. While we were "Teddy and the 3 Ks" in Evanston, the third K was nonexistent to them.

They betrayed their attitude toward me and what I represented for Teddy through their attempted involvement of Melissa's parents in our life in Evanston. Conservative Evangelicals, Melissa's parents - urged on by Matthew - called Teddy on a February Saturday and spent the better part of an hour-long conversation condemning him and me, berating him for betraying their dead daughter, and threatening him with legal action if he insisted on raising Melissa's children in a "sinful environment" that was "not Biblical." Unless Teddy returned to the "straight" and narrow, they wanted the Ks to live with them, and they wanted Melissa's trust fund restored with them as trustees and Teddy's boys as sole beneficiaries.

I learned all of this later that day, as Teddy had taken the call in the kitchen but - when it was clear it was headed south - had moved into the office and closed the door behind him to ensure neither I nor the Ks overheard it. When it was over, Teddy was silent. But, it was clear he was troubled; his blue eyes were flat, and he either would not or could not smile. At times like these, I knew not to press or pry. Teddy would come to me when he was ready. Until then, he would brood, lost in his own thoughts and trying to digest or work out whatever the issues was.

When the Ks left for basketball, Teddy brought me into the loop. I was shocked. After all, it was 2018, the gay marriage issue was settled nationally (and had been for 2 years), and atavistic views like those of Melissa's parents had, for the most part, been shamed into the closet.

After assuring Teddy he need not fret about custody of the Ks or actions on the trust, I asked "What did you say to them?"

"They're the boys' only grandparents, what could I say?" Teddy asked, reminding me his parents had died years before.

"You could them to fuck off, to mind their own business, to stop invoking the ghost of their dead daughter in the name of controlling things they have no say in."

Teddy blanched at my mention of "their dead daughter." Then, he glared at me, showing he thought I had crossed a line.

"I could have. But, I have things to worry about that you don't, namely my boys."

I blanched at the exclusion. He, too, had crossed a line. Afraid we were headed down a dangerous path, I retreated.

"What brought this all up today?"

"I assume it was Matthew. They would never have known otherwise. I certainly didn't tell them. I haven't told anyone."

Teddy inadvertently stoked a burgeoning resentment. While he seemed fine with our life in Evanston, he did not seem fine with it anywhere else. His brother and sister had no idea he even lived with me, even when they pressed him to explain why he had moved from Spain to Evanston instead of someplace where he had family, or at least someplace sunny and warm like the coast of Spain had been. So, Teddy was fully integrated into my life; my friends and family knew him and accepted him. But, I was not remotely integrated into his life; I had not met a single friend of his or either of his siblings. With Teddy reeling from the call with Melissa's parents, I should have subordinated my pique. I did not. Instead, I turned and left the room. Already dressed for a run, I took off before Teddy could reign me back in, just as I had in Jackson all those years before. I cried as I ran. It was cathartic.

When I got back from my run, Teddy was napping in our bed, a Cardinals throw draped over his naked body. Teddy was on his stomach with his arms crossed above his head, which was turned to the right. As I sat in a chair removing my running shoes, I stared at him. Even after all this time, I found him breathtaking. He did not shave often, so his cheeks were stubbled. He slept with a slight smile on his face. His hairy armpit was visible to me, as was his the right nipple and hairy chest. The muscles on his back rippled, even at rest. The throw covered his ass and the tops of his legs, but his hairy calves and athletic feet were visible.

I loved looking at him. My dick twitched almost every time I did, especially when he was naked. I was not one to believe sex cured all ills. But, it certainly did not hurt them, either. So, I stripped out of my running clothes and moved toward him. I pulled the throw off of him and climbed onto the bed, hovering over him. I kissed the back of his neck as he woke up.

"What are you doing?"

"Fucking you," I said as I licked down his back. He spread his legs as I moved my tongue down the crack of his ass. I loved eating his ass, and I proved it, burying my face and rimming the hell out of him. His moans and movements validated my efforts.

I moved to his inner thighs, licking them as I moved down his legs to his feet. I licked the arches of his feet, teased the balls of his feet with my teeth, and alternately sucked his toes and licked between them.

I worked my way back up his legs, pulling his dick and balls back between them so my tongue had access to both. I licked the underside of his dick. I licked and sucked his balls. I licked his taint. I rimmed him again.

As he pushed back into me, I penetrated him with my tongue. His groans and movements invited more, so I kneeled behind him, took him by the hips, and slowly entered him. He inhaled deeply as I pushed into him as deeply as I could. He clenched his ass, holding me still and tight. I lowered myself to him, hooked my arms under his, and buried my face in his neck. He hooked his ankles around mine, so we were as entwined as we could be. It was perfectly intimate.

"I love you, Kevin."

"I love you, too, Teddy."

"Then fuck me."

"I'm trying, but your ass won't let me."

He chuckled and loosened his grip. I fucked him slowly, pulling out as far as I could without leaving him before pushing back in. My pace was glacial, almost like I was trying not to make a sound. I loved the feeling of his velvety ass around my dick. I do not know how long I fucked him like that, but it seemed like forever. Every time I got close, I backed off.

I needed to kiss him, but doing so was not easy in this position. I did not want to, but I pulled out of him and rolled him onto his back. He raised his legs in the air, and I hooked my arms under them. I re-entered him and then lowered my mouth to his. I kissed him as deeply as I could. He held my head in with his hands as I did. As we kissed, he clenched and unclenched my dick with his ass. Combined with the depth and breadth of our still unbroken kiss, the sensation of his ass working my dick started to overwhelm me.

"I'm getting close."

He let go of my dick, and I started fucking him with purpose. He let go of my head, but we maintained the kiss. He grabbed my ass and drove me in as deeply as he could. I came as he did. He used his ass muscles to milk me dry. Our lips never touched each other.

When we finally broke, Teddy's chest hair was slick with our sweat, and I smelled like a goat. I had not showered, had gone for a long run, and then had gone for a marathon fuck. I pulled out of Teddy and whispered "I need a shower" in his ear.

"Me, too."

In the shower, Teddy kissed me again as the water ran over both of us. It was another deep, long kiss. I ran my hands through his chest hair and around to his ass. I pulled his hard dick into my stomach. I lowered my head to his right nipple, sucked it, and then moved to the left. I kissed his stomach and then took his beautiful dick into my mouth. I started to suck him, wanting desperately to taste his cum. But, Teddy had other ideas. He stopped me and pulled me back up, kissing me again.

When he broke the kiss, Teddy turned me around and positioned my hands against the shower wall. I was standing as if I was about to be searched. I expected Teddy to fuck me. I wanted Teddy to fuck me. I needed needed to fuck me.

He did not. Instead, he filled his hands with shampoo and slowly washed my hair. Then, he used body wash to slowly, gently, softly clean my entire body. It was sensuous and lovely. As he caressed my chest and stomach from behind, he rubbed his chest against my back and his hard dick against my ass. I pushed back again, trying to force him to fuck me. He resisted, slid between my legs from behind, leaned his back against the shower wall, and took my dick into his mouth. He gripped my ass and fucked his face with my dick. He went all the way down, his soft tongue working the sweet spot under my head. I came fast and hard. He used his throat to milk me dry again.

I was spent, having come twice - hard - in short order.
Teddy was not. As I rested against the wall, he moved behind me and started eating me out. When he had had his fill, he stood and finally started to push into me. I pushed back. I was tired,

but I also wanted - needed - to hold him inside me. We had not sexed like this in a long time, and I did not want it to be over.

Teddy entered me easily, then took my hips in his hands, steadied me, and started fucking me. He had been hard for a long time, and I could tell he needed to come.

"Fuck me harder," I demanded, urging him on. He did, slamming in and out of me with abandon. He grunted as he came. I could feel him filling me. It was one of my favorite feelings.

Teddy could not or would not stop. He stayed hard and kept fucking me, his cum working as lube in my sore ass. Quickly, he came again, his grunt just as loud and as deep as the first one. He put his face to my back and relaxed, holding me as he did.

When he pulled out of me, I turned my back to the wall and slid down to the corner. I was emotionally drained and physically exhausted. Teddy collapsed onto the shower floor next to me, pressed his forehead to mine, and put his hand to the back of my head. I locked my arms around him, and put my chin to his shoulder. I do not know how long we stayed like that, but the warm water and the love washed over both of us.

I wanted to sleep. I used Teddy to steady myself, then pulled him to his feet. We stepped out of the shower, barely rubbed a towel over our bodies, and went to bed wet. Teddy laid on his back, and I laid next to him with my head on his shoulder and my hand in his chest hair. We were both quickly asleep.

Part Thirteen

Kyle shook me awake.

"It's late, and we're hungry." I opened my eyes to find the Ks staring at me. I raised up and looked at the clock. It was 8:47, and the Ks had not had dinner. I shook Teddy awake.

"We need to make dinner." Teddy looked at the clock and bolted up.

"It's late."

"Yes, and the boys are hungry."

"So am I."

Teddy looked to Kurt and Kyle and told them to go downstairs and get the eggs and pancake batter and bacon out of the refrigerator. "We're having breakfast for dinner."

When they had cleared out, Teddy and I quickly slipped into shorts and t-shirts. I stopped him as he headed toward the stairs, pulled him into me, and apologized into his chest.

"I'm sorry about earlier."

"I know. And, I know we have some things to work through. But, I can't fight you, Melissa's parents, and my boys all at the same time. I need someone on my side."

We held hands as we headed downstairs to the kitchen. We listened to Sinatra as we made breakfast dinner. We ate in the family room while we watched some mindless movie that 12 years olds find hilarious when they are twelve and that does not stand the test of time when they re-watch it later. Teddy sat in his chair, and we three Ks sat on the sofa. When we were done eating, the boys snuggled into me. I put my arms around each of them, and they burrowed into my chest.

I had never wanted to be a parent. After all, I had found a cat overwhelming. But, I was overwhelmed by how deeply the Ks had insinuated themselves into my heart and my psyche. I ached for them when I was at the office, and I thought about them whenever they were not around. I could not imagine how Teddy had sent the "candy boys" to New England; the Ks had been around only a few months, and I could not have survived sending them away. They were too important to me.

Teddy and I had been concerned they would miss their older brothers terribly, but they seemed to be happy to be out of the shadows and finally catching some sun. They no longer had to defer to M&M, and they were becoming more confident and assertive in their absence. I adored them, and - to my great surprise - they adored me. They did not fear my judgment as much as they feared their father's, so they shared bits with me that they did not share with him. Often, the three of us would laugh conspiratorially or share looks and smiles that suggested Teddy was the lone adult on Hastings. When we watched TV, they snuggled up to me. When they needed advice, they came to me. I was their conspirator and confidante and, sometimes when Teddy was out, their confessor.

We had kept the Ks out of school for the Spring semester as well. Teddy decided to home school them. We would start them in 8th grade the following Fall.

Time marched to the beat of our routine. When Teddy explained to Melissa's parents that their feelings on his life were inconsequential other than jeopardizing access they to their grandchildren, they decided to suppress their judgment, at least in their dealings with Teddy. I am sure it did not hurt that it was by now clear to them that if Kurt and Kyle had to choose between them and me, they were sure losers.

Teddy told his siblings why he was in Evanston. Their reaction was confused. They loved their brother, but his marriage to Melissa was an obstacle to their understanding of us and what we were doing. For whatever reason, they could not get their arms around Teddy's new normal, even though they had known me way back when Teddy was Atreyu and I was "dork."

Kurt and Kyle turned 13 on April 20. To celebrate, we took them to the Cardinals/Cubs game that night at Wrigley Field. We sat Teddy, Kurt, Kevin, Kyle. The boys seemed jittery, and not just from too much soda and way too much cotton candy. They kept glancing at me, glancing at their dad, and then glancing at the scoreboard. If it had not been so furtive, then I'm not sure I'd have noticed. But, they were acting like they were on drugs.

During the 5th inning change-over, I discovered their "drug." As the grounds crew swept the field, the P.A. announcer interrupted the slight buzz of the crowd, "Kevin Michaels. Kevin Michaels. Please turn your attention to the jumbotron in center field."

I had heard my name, but the instructions had not registered. Kurt and Kyle grabbed my arms and snapped me out of my ignorance.

"Kevin, Kevin, Kevin, look at the jumbotron . . . look at the jumbotron!!"

I followed their fingers. The jumbotron bore a simple message: "I want to marry you."

I furrowed my brow. I did not understand what was going on. I turned to Teddy. He was down on one knee with his hand out. I put my hand in his, and he said "I want to marry you."

I felt thousands of eyes on me. When I said "I want to marry you more," Teddy stood up and wrapped his arms around me. As I wrapped my arms around him, the crowd - at least the part that mattered to me - erupted. As Teddy kissed me, Kurt and Kyle jumped on us from behind. Both of them were hanging from my neck as Teddy engulfed the three of us and buried his face in ours. We were a bundle of pure joy, and we all started to cry. The Cubs played Train's "Marry me" over the P.A. system.

I choked "I love you, Teddy" through my tears. He choked "backatcha" through his. The Ks were too overwhelmed to say anything. I have no idea how long we stayed huddled like that, but it was certainly too long. When we finally separated, the folks in our section were still standing and still applauding. The world had changed dramatically in the last 15 years, from the scare-mongering of 2004 to the validating cheers a stadium of Cubbies.

I was too drunk on emotion to stay for the rest of the game. We headed home. As we did, Kurt spoke for Kyle.

"Kevin, you can choose either me or Kyle for your best man. Dad gets stuck with the other one."

I did not even think of Thom or any of my other friends. "I cannot choose between the two of you. So, you can just switch sides halfway through."

"Awesome," said Kyle. "I told you he wouldn't pick you," he said, glaring at Kurt.

We were all holding hands - Teddy, Kurt, Kyle, and Kevin - as we walked to the train. I had never been happier. I had the love of a good man. Correction, I had the love of a great man. Correction, I had the love of three great men.

Part Fourteen

Although marriage was legal everywhere, we decided to get married in Ogunquit, Maine, the second weekend of June. I loved Ogunquit. I had been going there since 2000, spending a long Fall weekend at the Beachmere Inn, Five-O Shore Road, MC's, Amore, and the Front Porch.

Teddy had stalled in telling the "candy boys." When he finally did, their reaction was predictable. They were appalled and insisted they would not attend. I no longer cared, but their father certainly did. The rupture was deepening. As we lay in bed that night, I told Teddy I did not need to marry him, if it was going to further the breach between him and the M&M.

"I am not going to let them determine my happiness," he insisted, indignantly.

"I'm just saying . . . . I know what we have and what we are . . . . And I know it's forever. I don't need some state's imprimatur to confirm that, especially if it is going to make M&M hate me more."

Teddy chuckled. "Like that's possible."

I was wounded, but I tried not to show it. I looked Teddy in the eyes. "We don't have to do this."

"Yes, we do. It's important to me. It's important to Kurt and Kyle. In fact, it was their idea."

"What do you mean?"

"Kurt raised it. I was in bed next to him months ago, and he said 'You should marry Kevin.' I asked 'You think so,' and he responded 'I know so.' I had not really thought about it before, at least not in any kind of concrete way, but I realized then and there that he was right."

"He was right."

We did not talk about M&M again. We knew they were isolating themselves, but we figured they had to work through this on their own. If we pushed, they would only push back.

* * * * *

The four of us flew to Boston on June 7 and then headed up the coast to Ogunquit. Our guest list was limited: my clerks, my assistant, my decrepit parents, Thom and a small group of my Chicago friends, Teddy's sister and her family, and Teddy's brother and his family. Invited and missing: M&M and Melissa's parents. M&M were boycotting out of intolerance. Melissa's parents may have preferred to be, but we knew they were too infirm to travel. Their days were measured in weeks, not months.

It rained all day on June 8. Not regular rain. Sideways rain.

That night, we took the second floor of MC's in the Cove and had a perfect evening. Everyone was excited and got along. We carried our revelry down Shore Road to the Front Porch for showtunes. We talked Kurt and Kyle in, even though they were only 13. We had a blast.

On Saturday, we awoke to more rain. We were supposed to get married at 6 p.m. on the lawn by the Marginal Way, but we could not defy the rain. Just after lunch, the rain stopped. The sky was still grey, but at least it was not open.

My family showed up at 4 for pictures. Teddy and I wore tan seersucker suits with orange ties, his traditional and mine bowed, and orange orchids on our lapels.

After pictures, we headed to the fire pit for drinks with our guests. It was raucous and electric.

Just before six, Teddy, Kurt, and Kyle and I joined hands and headed down the hill to the site. The string quartet welcomed us with Etta James' "At Last." Just as we took our place before the arbor, the sun came out. It was either serendipity or a sign. I took it as a sign.

As our first act, we lit candles for Melissa, Teddy's mom and dad, and my little sister, who had died years before in a car accident.

Then, we read poems to each other. I started with W.H. Auden's "If I Could Tell You," slightly modified:

Time will say nothing but I told you so,

Time only knows the price we have to pay;

If I could tell you I would let you know.

If we should weep when clowns put on their show,

If we should stumble when musicians play,

Time will say nothing but I told you so.

There are no fortunes to be told, although,

131

Because I love you more than I can say,

If I could tell you I would let you know.

The winds must come from somewhere when they blow,

There must be reasons why the leaves decay;

Time will say nothing but I told you so.

Perhaps the roses really want to grow,

The vision seriously intends to stay;

If I could tell you I would let you know.

Suppose all the lions get up and go,

And all the brooks and soldiers run away;

I will always love you more than I can say.

Time will say nothing but I told you so.

Teddy followed with Sonnett 116:

Let me not to the marriage of true minds

Admit impediments. Love is not love

Which alters when it alteration finds,

Or bends with the remover to remove,

O no! it is an ever-fixed mark

That looks on tempests and is never shaken;

It is the star to every wand'ring bark,

Whose worth's unknown, although his height be taken,

Love's not Time's fool, though rosy lips and cheeks

Within his bending sickle's compass come;

Lover alters not with his brief hours and weeks,

But bears it out even to the edge of doom.

If this be error and upon me prov'd,

I never writ, nor no man ever lov'd.

Kurt and Kyle switched sides before we followed with our personal vows. I started.

Before you, I was in love with the promise of you.

With you, I am in love with the promise of us.

I promise to spend our married life becoming the man

you see when you look at me.

I promise to spend our married life becoming the man who

deserves who I see when I look at you.

I promise to spend our married life loving you with all my heart.

Always and forever.

I promise.

Teddy followed:

Kevin, today is a very special day.

I get to marry you: The person I love more than anyone else.

30 years ago you were just a fantasy, an ideal.

But here I am: Marrying just that person.

You make me happy.

You support me, you challenge me to be a better person,

you have taught me how to love.

We have waited such a long time for this, and now that we are here,

I get to promise to be your friend and life partner no matter

what life brings to us.

I am so looking forward to spending the rest of my life with you,

caring for you, nurturing you, being there for you in all life

has for us, and I pledge my commitment to you,

secure in the knowledge that you will be my constant friend,

and my one true love.

We exchanged rings and promised eternal love. I cried as we did.

When the ceremony was over, we had a brilliant dinner at the Beachmere. We laughed about what was, we cried about what wasn't, and we tried to figure out the gap between. Kurt and Kyle seemed to be the happiest of all of us, and that made me happier than I had ever been.

When the night had run its course, Teddy and I retired to our room. There was no novelty, only familiarity. But, even the familiar can be different. We had never made love as a married couple. That night we did.

I was on my back, and Teddy was hovering over me and kissing me and teasing me about being his "wife." I wanted to protest, but our positions left me, well, in the wife role.

We kissed and kissed and kissed as he hovered over me and I ran my hands over his smooth back and ass. Our future was apparent and evident in those kisses. I moved my hands to the hairy chest I loved so much. As I did, he pressed his hard dick at my taint. We both knew where this was headed, so I decided to end the suspense.

"Fuck me."

"Gladly, Ms. AAtreyu," he joked as he pressed his dick at my ass.

His Ms. AAtreyu made me want to turn the tables.

"Never mind. Ride me, Ms. Michaels."

Teddy laughed as he called my bluff. "Gladly," he said as he positioned himself over my hard dick. As he slid down me, I gasped. His legs spread wide, he stayed perfectly upright, his hands on my stomach. In this position, I was able to rub his chest and stomach as he rode me. As I got close, I put my hands on his hip bones and tried to slow him down. I failed. He rode me fast and hard until I came powerfully in his ass. My head and back were arched off the bed as I did. I collapsed into the pillow, spent and sweaty.

Teddy pulled off and leaned over me, his beautiful dick in my face. No matter what I wanted, I wanted him in my mouth more. I cupped his ass and drove him in and out of my face. I opened my throat and took him all the way down. When I did, he exploded, filling my mouth and throat. I took all he had to offer. I refused to stop, sucking him until he could not take any more and had to pull out of my mouth.

Teddy collapsed onto me. I locked my legs around him and tried to pull him through me. I squeezed him as hard as I could until he pulled his head back and stared at me.

"I love you, husband."

"I love you, too, husband," I responded.

He kissed me. I kissed him back, trying to pour myself into him. When the kiss finally broke, we had almost nothing left. Teddy rolled off of me, and we turned into each other. I put my right hand around his neck, and he put his left hand around mine. We pulled each other close until our mouths and chests and dicks were touching. I took his big toe between my toes. He put his left leg over my legs.

I opened my mouth, and he pushed his tongue in. I circled his tongue with mine. I have no idea how long we kissed, but I was the one to break it.

"I still want you to fuck me."

"Gladly," he said.

I rolled onto my right side, and Teddy moved in behind me. He gripped me with his left arm as he pushed at my ass. I hooked my left leg around his, and pushed back into him. He bit my neck as he pushed at my ass. I rolled onto my stomach, pulling him on top of me. Quickly, I had both of his hands in mine, his head was in my neck, his chest and stomach were in my back, his dick was in my ass, and his feet were covering mine. We were two as one. We laid like that, neither of us moving, each of us soaking the other in, breathing in the same rhythm.

When I thought it could not get more intimate, Teddy started to move inside me, slowly pulling out and pushing back in. His thick dick paralyzed me with pleasure. I lay perfectly still as he fucked me, every part of our body touching that could. When he whispered he was close, I insisted he stop. When he pulled out of me, I rolled over, spread my legs, and wrapped them around him. He re-entered me. Our mouths met. As I hooked my legs around his, he started to move in and out of me again. I used my legs and arms to pull him closer. He sped up as he pressed his mouth to mine, his chest and stomach against mine. I whispered "make love to me" as he pushed in and out of me. We were moving as one. I was totally, completely at his mercy.

We went on like that, slowing down and speeding up to make it last as long as we could. Finally, I could not take any more, and I arched my back. Teddy read me perfectly, raised himself up, and started to drive into my more powerfully. I came, shooting arcs of cum over my stomach and chest and onto my face. Seeing me cum, Teddy could not resist. He filled me, his warm cum filling me as he stared into my eyes before collapsing onto me. We were soaked in sweat and covered in cum. I kissed his bald head. He raised his face to mine, and we kissed, deeply and truly. He licked some of the cum off my face, then kissed me again, letting me taste myself.

Teddy broke the kiss, falling off of me onto his right side. I rolled over to face him, pressing my lips to his. We fell asleep kissing . . . married . . . happy.

Part Fifteen

We took Kurt and Kyle and headed to the Amalfi coast for our honeymoon. We invited Matthew and Mark, but they, of course, declined. They'd rather eat a bucket of wet hair than spend two weeks with me in Italy. So, they stayed in New England with their friends/D.C. with Melissa's parents.

We loved the Amalfi coast, especially Positano. The four of us had a great trip. It was fueled by the euphoria of Maine, and Kurt and Kyle were riding the highest.

Our first night on the coast, we had two rooms. But, that was futile. Kurt and Kyle would not leave our room, so they slept with us in our bed. We all slept on our left sides . . . Teddy, me, Kurt, Kyle. My arms were long enough that I reached around both Kurt and Kyle.

The next day, we cancelled the Ks' room. There was no reason to waste the money; Kurt and Kyle were definitely staying with us. It was not the honeymoon I expected (Teddy and I were never alone), but it was the honeymoon I needed.

We stayed on the coast for two weeks. As our trip was coming to an end, I noticed that Teddy seemed thinner. I asked him about it.

"Are you losing weight?"

"No, why?"

"When I put my head on your chest, you seem thinner. I think you are losing weight."

It was a harmless observation. Five months later, I was alarmed. Teddy was thinner than I ever remembered, even though I knew he was working out daily. I addressed it at Thanksgiving, a holiday for which Mathew and Mark deigned to grace us with their presence.

It was Thanksgiving Eve, and Teddy and I had just made furtive love. We were coming down, and my head was on his chest. As I looked down him, he seemed skinny. Too skinny.

"Teddy, you are too thin."

"I can't keep weight on. I eat and work out and just get thinner."

"That's not right."

"I know."

"You need to go to the doctor."

"I know, but I'm scared."

"There's no reason to be."

I would turn out to be very wrong.

Matthew and Mark were borderline tolerable during their visit. It was clear Kurt and Kyle reveled in their presence. And, it was clear their father loved having them home, and they loved being with him. It was equally clear they did not enjoy me, and I did not enjoy them. In fact, I thought they were dicks. I'm sure they thought the same of me.

We dropped Matthew and Mark at Midway on Sunday. With their grumpiness toward me absent from the house, we had a great Sunday night. Kurt and Kyle were talkative at dinner, and we played Risk after. It had been my favorite game as a child, and I had taught the Ks to enjoy world domination.

Once the Ks were settled in their rooms, Teddy and I settled into ours. I could tell he was horny. While I was brushing my teeth, he pulled my boxers down and started licking my ass. When I leaned over to spit, he started rimming me. When I had had as much as I could take, I turned around and pulled Teddy to his feet. I sucked his nipples as I undid the tie on the scrubs he was wearing, freeing his now rock hard dick. My tongue followed his path to paradise. I licked the precum from his piss slit and took him in my mouth. I took him to the base and started milking him. I could feel him getting close, but he stopped me and pulled me up. He kissed me and led me to our bed. Once there, he worked us into a 69 and we started sucking each other in rhythm. We had not done this in ages, but we were still good at it. We came at the same time, filling each other's mouths. We both swallowed, but neither of us pulled off the other. We went soft in each other's mouths. I was almost asleep when I heard Teddy say "come up here." I did. He kissed me goodnight, and I fell asleep with my face in his chest.

The next morning, Teddy fucked me missionary style before the Ks banged on our door to rouse us. It was familiar, but still fantastic. We stared into each others eyes the entire time. Right after he came, he pulled out and took me in his mouth. I filled his throat almost immediately.

Teddy unlocked the door, slipped back into his scrubs, and tossed my boxers to me. The Ks predictably joined us in bed a few minutes later. They climbed in bed with us almost every morning, even if only long enough for us to say the Serenity Prayer as a group.

Once we got the Ks off to school, I went with Teddy to our doctor. We jointly discussed his weight loss. Then, Teddy surprised my by mentioning recurring back pain I had never heard about before.

We were there way longer than I expected. I had a feeling of foreboding when we left. They had run test after test after test. They had not said anything remotely optimistic. They seemed to be cushioning us, at least in retrospect. I think they knew what was coming and tried very hard not to alarm us until they were sure.

They called us back in later that week, and we heard words no one should ever hear in the same sentence . . . cancer . . . pancreas . . . advanced. Pancreatic cancer is awful. When they find it early-which almost never happens-the victim has little chance. When they find it late-as they had with Teddy-the victim has no chance.

Our once bright future was now not bright at all. It was dark, clouded and shrouded by Teddy's unavoidable and imminent death.

We tried to shield the Ks, but we could not. They were smart and perceptive and incisive and knew the mood on Hastings had changed dramatically. But, we did not know how to tell them. They had lost one parent to cancer, and now they were going to lose another to the same dreaded disease.

With no good option, we decided to be as direct as we could. Of course, they were afraid and they cried. Once they knew, the three of us cried and cried and cried together, shielding their father whenever we could but overwhelming each other with our shared grief.

We did not try to shield Matthew and Mark. We brought them into the loop immediately. Like the Ks, they were shattered. The truth was revealed; they were happy to be rebels so long as their rebellion bore little or no consequence. Their tone and attitude changed immediately.

The six of us had a somber, joyless Christmas. But, the break brought us all closer together. Matthew and Mark moved past their resentment of me and enjoyed their father and brothers.

Teddy wanted things to stay as normal as they could. I did not. I convinced him not to send M&M back to New Hampshire for the Spring semester. I thought they should spend whatever time their father had left with him.

I also took a leave of absence from the bench. I'd have been a useless judge in any event, my heart and mind wandering elsewhere when I should have been focused on the litigants and the issues before me.

We spent our days together, pretending through games of Monopoly and Risk and Trivial Pursuit that we were not engaged in a long, sad good-bye.

Teddy did not last long. He wasted, his body leaving us long before his mind.

He died in our house in February. It was the middle of the night, so I was the only one with him.

I was curled up beside him in bed. He was emaciated. He was no longer Teddy.

I held his bony body. I told him I loved him more than I had ever loved anyone or anything. I cried into his neck.

I felt his labored breathing. I felt his last labored breath.

I held him. He was gone, but I held him. He was dead, but I held him.

Our life together was over, but I held him.

Part Sixteen

I had to tell his boys. I probably should have told them when it happened, but I could not. I wanted that experience all to myself. I was selfish.

I pulled away from what was Teddy and got dressed. I put on his scrubs and my red tank. Then, I went into M&M's room. It was empty.

I went into the Ks' room. The four of them were camped out on the floor, between the beds. It was a beautiful sight-four brothers who loved each other deeply-and I had to shatter it with terrible news.

I decided to play it slow. I crawled into the foursome. I sat with my back against the bed. Kurt and Kyle stirred and put their heads in my lap. I stroked their hair.

Matthew was the first to wake up. He sat up and looked at me and knew. He cried, and I did, too. Matthew shook Mark awake. Matthew's tears betrayed what had happened. Mark sat up, buried his face in Matthew's shoulder, and started to sob.

Kurt and Kyle woke up. I pulled them into me.

I choked out "your dad's gone" between my own sobs. Kurt and Kyle cried into my shoulders. Matthew and Mark moved toward us and buried themselves in their brothers. I wrapped my arms around as much of them as I could. We were united in our grief. We cried until we could not cry any more. Then, we just huddled silently, not wanting the reality of Teddy's death to register as it would when we broke our huddle and started dealing with what we wanted to pretend had not happened.

* * * * *

With all of the notice, Teddy left little for us to do. We cremated his body and planned to fulfill his wish of being sprinkled in the ocean of Ogunquit. We had a small gathering for our friends and for Teddy's brother and sister and their families.

Teddy's sister brought notes from him for each of us. As was typical of Teddy, the notes were brief and pointed. Teddy was not a writer. Mine said only "Thank you for the second chance. Please take care of our boys. They need you." "Our" was only three letters, but those three letters were so important to me.

The boys' was a joint note. It said only "You were the best part of my life. I am sorry to leave you. Please take care of Kevin. He needs you."

Teddy's estate bound us together even more than his death had, as he left me a substantial lump sum and a trust that paid an annual income to me and then vested in the boys when I died. The annual income was multiples of what I earned as a judge.

I worked with Matthew to plan a life after Teddy for the five of us. I figured the only way Matthew and I would peacefully co-exist was if we were partners, and he did not feel like I was trying to parent him or to replace either of his lost parents.

I figured right. Matthew and I had long talks about Kurt and Kyle and what they would need from me, him, and Mark moving forward. They had lost a lot in their brief lives, and I insisted to Matthew that they could not and should not endure a schism between the most important people left for them, namely me and the M's. Matthew agreed. The last brick fell.

I told Matthew I thought I should resign my judgeship. I also told him I thought we should leave our house and Evanston. I wanted a fresh start in a new place where the hint of Teddy did not lurk in every corner, reminding us all of what we had loved and lost.

I did not know where to go. It was liberating to be able to go anywhere, but it was also overwhelming. I like options, but too many options can be paralyzing.

Kurt offered the best solution. He wanted to go to Costa Rica, as he had read that Costa Ricans were the happiest people in the world. And, he thought we needed to be in the easiest place there was to be happy. So, Costa Rica it was. We used Rosetta

Stone and a private tutor to learn Spanish and made some scouting trips. We settled on Makanda, in the rain forest above Quepos.

We bought a beautiful house with a pool and prepared to move. Before we did, we went to Maine for a weekend to say a final good-bye to Teddy. We each had a share of his ashes, and we each said good-bye in our own way. The boys flung their shares high into the breeze and watched them disperse quickly. I sprinkled mine into the waves and watched them slowly drift away.

It had been hardest telling Thom we were leaving. With Teddy gone, he was my longest friend, having been with me for law school at Northwestern, where he now taught Antitrust and other classes. We had tried being together once, early on. But, it had not been right, at least not for me. I was still young and had not moved past Teddy, and we had not tried again when Teddy receded over the years. We were best friends, but that was it.

Thom had been a rock through Teddy's illness and death. I had to be strong for the boys and Teddy, but I could be weak with Thom. I cried into his ear too many nights when we both should have been asleep and not on our mobiles. He was a great listener, and he knew not to offer the usual pablum about it all being alright that folks tend to offer in tragic times when they do not know what else to say.

Thom was angry when I told him we were leaving. Oddly so. Still, he helped me ship our lives from Evanston to Makanda, and he accompanied us to the airport when we left. We both cried at security when we had to part. In 18 months, my life had transformed: I had gone from a single, professional man living alone in downtown Chicago to a wealthy "father" of four living in a foreign land.

*****

We settled relatively easily into life in Makanda. Of course, money makes a transition like that far simpler than it would otherwise be.

The boys decided they all wanted to go to the same school. We found a private one that catered to expats. It was pretty far from our home, but I trusted Matthew's and Mark's driving skills, even over the winding Costa Rican roads.

I thought we would be too busy to get lonely, but I was wrong. While I enjoyed the boys very much, I longed for adult company, especially when the boys were in school.

I invited Thom for Christmas. After various fits and starts, he ended up coming from December 3 (his last exam was December 2) to December 23. That way, we'd get a long visit, but he'd still be in Nashville with his parents for Christmas.

Thom's arrival finally brought some familiarity to my life. It was like finding an old sweater.

His first night, Thom fell asleep outside in a chaise. I thought of leaving him there overnight, but I feared it would startle him to wake up outside in the middle of the night. I ushered him to the guest room. While I was tucking him in, he asked me to stay with him until he was back asleep. I crawled into bed next to him, and he put his head against my shoulder. I woke up like that hours later, still in my jeans and fleece pullover. I looked over at Thom. His blonde hair had partied while we slept, and he had drooled on his pillow. Still, he was adorable, his sleeping, placid face innocent and untroubled.

I slid my arm out from under him and headed to my room. I did not want the boys to find us in the same bed, innocent or not.

Thom's visit raced by. We slept and read and ate and drank and took long walks and even longer naps. It is amazing how much time doing nothing can take.

I was sad to see him go. To my surprise, so were the boys. Thom had always made friends easily, and he was no different with the boys.

Christmas Eve, Matthew and I were the last two up. We were silently wrapping gifts and drinking wine together. Matthew broke the silence.

"Did you and Thom sleep together while he was here?"

I was stunned by the question. And, I was not sure it was any of his business, But, I also knew there were only two answers to that question: "no" and everything else, all of which would be interpreted as "yes."

"No."

"Why not?"

"We're not like that with each other?"

"Were you ever?"

"A long time ago. Briefly. But not really."

"What happened?"

"We were young, and I was still pining for your father. I spent most of my youth-including all of college and law school-waiting, hoping, praying for your father and closing myself to others because they were not him."

The silence returned. Matthew broke it again.

"We think you should."

"Should what? And, who is 'we'?"

"Sleep with Thom. All of us. We talked about it. We like Thom, and he likes us. And, it's clear he likes you. You should like him."

"He does not like me like that."

"Yes, he does."

I talked to Thom later that night. As we were every year, we were on the phone when Christmas Eve turned to Christmas Day, at least in Thom's time zone. I relayed the odd conversation with Matthew from earlier that night.

"They're right," Thom said. "I do like you . . . . like that."

I was caught off-guard. "Since when?"

"Since forever."

"Why didn't you ever say anything?"

"I did. We dated. But, you were looking backward to Teddy, not forward with me. Or with anyone else for that matter. So, it didn't work. Then, we settled into a great friendship. I was certain it would develop into more at some point, but you wouldn't let it. There was just no room for anyone else, and I wanted a lover, not a fuck buddy. I settled for a friend. A great friend."

"Gosh, Thom, I never knew."

"Of course you didn't. I was not going to give you that kind of power. Or, that kind of burden. It would have gotten in the way."

As we often did, we stayed on the phone, listening to each other breathe. I fell asleep. Thom woke me up, "Merry Christmas, Kevin. I love you."

"Merry Christmas to you, Thommy. I love you, too."

The boys and I had a joyous Christmas on the public beach near the national park. The beach was packed. The people-especially the children-were joyful. So were we.

I thought of Teddy a lot throughout the day. But, I also thought of Thom, reviewing our years of friendship through the hindsight of the conversation of the night before.

In February, we had a simple ceremony to mark the anniversary of Teddy's death. I had asked each boy to choose their favorite picture of their father, and I had them matted and framed together in birth order, one copy for each of them (and one for myself, although I did not tell them that). For the top picture, Matthew chose a picture of Teddy alone, looking away from the camera, deep in thought. It was essential Teddy.

For the second picture, Mark chose one of Teddy, him, and Matthew from the trip that took them away to school. They were all leaning against the car and posed the same way, like hoodlums in the modern day.

For the third and fourth pictures, Kurt and Kyle wanted to choose pictures of the four of us from the wedding. But, I convinced them to choose something else, afraid the wedding pictures would make M&M regretful for choosing to skip it. So, Kurt chose a picture I had taken of him and his dad as Teddy snapped a selfie of the two of them. It was a beautiful, whimsical picture.

And, Kyle chose a picture of Teddy and me from our trip to the Amalfi coast. It was not a great picture, but I think Kyle wanted me represented in the collection.

Once they opened their "gifts," I had each boy write down their favorite memories of their father, fold the papers on which they were written neatly into an envelope, and tape their envelope to the back of their gifts for safekeeping. I explained that, years from now, they would discover the memory envelope-maybe when unpacking a box or when moving to a new house-open it, and be reminded of their father. And, they would smile, reminded of what was and what should have been.

We had learned a lot in the year since Teddy died. We had learned that grief does not end, it just changes. We had learned that grief was not a place, but a process. We had learned that, while we'd have given anything to have Teddy with us, we were better people-toward each other and toward others-for having experienced and survived his death. And, we had learned that we needed each other. A lot.

*****

I invited Thom down for his Spring Break. We did not discuss whether the invitation was for more than a visit, and I was not sure if it was or it wasn't. I cautioned the boys against thinking it was more than a visit, but-of course-their imaginations galloped ahead of the facts.

When Thom arrived, Kyle took his bag to my room, not to the guest room. When I told him to move it, Matthew smiled and said "Let's wait and see."

Thom and I were the last ones up, again outside in the lounge chairs. I raised the subject.

"Kyle put your things in my room."

"What do you think about that?"

"Seems aggressive."

"We can share a bed without anything happening. We have gobs of times over the years."

"I know. But, those times, there was not even a possibility of something happening. So, the situation was not fraught."

"Thanks."

"You know what I mean."

"Yes, I have known for 25 years."

"About that, why didn't you make your desires more clear."

"I couldn't compete with the possibility of Teddy. A ghost is one thing. A ghost can't return and spoil things. But, a possibility is quite another. A possibility can crash the party at any time."
I understood what he was saying. No matter the state of my life or my commitment to another, I'd have abandoned it all and fled to Teddy and his "Have you ever been to Spain" inquiry. Nothing would or could have kept me from Teddy.

Thom interrupted my thoughts. "Look, I love you, and you love me. I think you are the love of my life, but I know I am not the love of your life. But, I think I could be a love of your life, and that's enough for me."

I looked at Thom's gentle face. I did love him. Very much. I had spent half my life relying on him, consoling him, gossiping to him, and listening to him breathe into the other end of my mobile.

"Let's go to bed," I said, as I finished my wine and stood up.

"Together?"

"Why not? We've done it countless times."

In my room, Thom stripped to his boxer briefs and climbed into Teddy's side of the bed. Thom was not my type. Generally, I was attracted to dark hair, dark eyes, and a decent amount of body hair. Thom was the opposite of all those things. He had fine blonde hair that he parted on the side and kept cut above his ears and off his neck. I wanted a rough look, and Thom looked like an altar boy. He had an innocent face, noteworthy mostly for the whites of his blue eyes. They were like milk, the whitest I had ever seen, unmarred by veins or red. He had large white teeth and a great smile, even if it was a bit crooked. He was a tennis player, so he had a tennis player's build. His muscles were long and sinewy. He had a tuft of blonde hair on his chest, but not much. He had a small path of blonde hair that trailed from his navel into his boxers. He had a lot of moles. I had never seen his dick.

I climbed into my side of the bed. It was odd to be in bed with someone other than Teddy or the boys. It made me a little melancholy.

We were face to face. Thom's hands were at his chest, and I took them into mine. I put my face to his and whispered, "I just want to listen to you breathe."

Thom kissed me, pulled my hands to his chest, and put his forehead to mine. "Let's sleep." He knew me perfectly.

Part Seventeen

Thom and I slept together the entire week, but we did not sex each other. We never had, and-for whatever reason-I was not ready for it. But, I was ready for the intimacy that preceded sex. So, we kissed, nuzzled, held hands and each other, spooned on the lounge chairs and in bed, and generally touched each other a lot. Before the week was over, Thom was planning to spend the summer with us.

Kurt had been right. Costa Rica was a happy place, and we were happy there. When we needed more than each other, we headed to the public beach or to Cafe Milagro, at the top of the hill.

The boys seemed as excited by Thom's pending return as I was. They thought the summer would be a "dry run" and, if it went well, then Thom would become a permanent in our home. I was not so sure. The ghost of Teddy hung over me, and no amount of

162

rationality could purge it from my thoughts. Still, the hint of love was in the air. I just was not sure I could take the hint.

There was no surprise when Thom arrived. I took him and his bags to my room. I pulled him into an embrace and told him I was glad he was there. Then, I left him alone to unpack, clean up, and settle in.

Over dinner, I watched Thom and the boys with each other. Thom was a natural with them, and their affection for him-including Matthew's-was obvious.

Watching them together resolved my hesitation. It was clear we fit together as a family. The only question was whether Thom and I could fit together as a couple. I decided to find out.

While the boys cleaned up the kitchen, I asked Thom if I could talk to him privately. He looked at me quizzically, but said sure. We went to my room. After I closed the door behind us, I took him into my arms, pressed my mouth to his, and kissed him as deeply as I could, replacing the gentleness of our Spring Break kisses with a hunger that shocked me.

Thom was taller than me and, disappointingly, stronger. He was also probably hungrier. He quickly dominated the kiss, pushing his tongue into my mouth and his body into mine. Thom moved me to the bed and started to undress me. He quickly had me naked and in his mouth. I had not been sexed for almost 18 months, and masturbation is no substitute for a good blow job. And, his was a good blow job, long and deep. I quickly came in Thom's mouth. After draining me, Thom smiled at me and told me I tasted as good as he expected.

I wanted Thom to fuck me, and I let him know by grabbing his belt, undoing it, unbuttoning his Levi's, ripping his zipper down, and laying back on the bed.

"I don't have a condom."

"I don't care. I trust you."

Thom pulled me to the edge of the bed and pulled my legs up over his shoulders. He used his spit for lube. He had a bigger cock than I expected, bigger even than Teddy's. I had regained some resistance, so it took some effort to make the sex happen. We exerted the effort, and Thom was inside me. I felt his hair against my ass as he pressed all the way in and paused so I could relax and adjust to him. I looked into his eyes, and he looked back into mine. We did not break eye contact as he slowly pulled back and pushed back in, over and over, gradually picking up the pace as his orgasm built against my prostate. As he got closer, he used his shoulders to push my legs to my shoulders, and he bent over and kissed me. He panted he loved me as he came, filling me. When he did, I came all over my abdomen and stomach. I grabbed Thom's face, pressing my mouth to his and demanding that his tongue probe the depths of my mouth.

"I love you, too, Thommy. I really do."

"I'm glad," he responded. "I really am."

The doubts were settled. Thom's "dry run" was supposed to last 6 weeks, but it was settled in 6 hours. He would resign his tenured professorship at NULS. He would sell his awesome Lake Shore condo and his BMW. He would move to Makanda, share my bed, share our house, and share responsibility for Matthew, Mark, Kurt, and Kyle. He would live with the ghost of Teddy, but he would not have to live with the possibility of Teddy. He would have to live only with the possibility of Kevin and Thom.

Explicit Erotic Sex Stories

Mark gets started(Gay)

Straight young men meet, begin to look all starry eyed at, fall away, and . . .

Pamela Vance

Chapter One

When I saw the blonde kid in Bryan Cave's library, I realized I needed him. I don't currently what it was, however it was substantial. I had set out to give up those days me, however he in a flash constrained me to think about inversion.

He looked so youthful, I figured he may be a secondary school kid running books for the lowest pay permitted by law. I thought wrong. He was Mason Raymond Davis, the solitary 1L the Cave recruited for that mid year.

I lifted my eyebrow and my hand to him as I strolled by. I felt his eyes on my back as I left.

Bricklayer - "Mace" for short - obviously didn't have the foggiest idea how alluring he was. He was too restrained, in both style and substance.

Be that as it may, he was frightfully appealing. He had thick light hair, green eyes with a conspicuous hover of orange around the students, and a brilliant however tricky grin that dimpled his cheeks to coordinate the dimple on his jawline.

His face was not half as appealing as his psyche. I had grown up advantaged. I went to St. Louis' Country Day School, at that

169

point to Yale, and afterward to the University of Chicago. I had consumed my time on earth around brilliant individuals. Mace was effectively the most intelligent. He saw and figured things I didn't.

I had no clue if Mace was keen on what I was keen on. However, I realized I needed to discover. I would need to play it gradually. One slip up could end my standing and my late spring.

My standing was principal, and I watched it passionately, particularly when I debilitated and hesitated with young men or men. It had begun my last year of secondary school, as graduation drew closer. Until that point, I had just played with the possibility that I may some time or another toy with a kid.

I was an entertainer. As a Senior, I got an enormous part in our Spring creation of The Breakfast Club. I had the Anthony Michael Hall job. Adam Samuels, likewise a Senior, had the Judd Nelson job.

Adam and I came from inverse sides. I struck a balance. I did nothing incorrectly. A Pisces, I was a 18 year old virgin. Not on the grounds that I needed chance, but since I was an acknowledged traditionalist and moralist.

My traditionalism appeared in my appearance. I appeared as though I could be President of the Young Republicans. I wore my earthy colored hair short, separated on the right. I had silver glasses. I wore white oxfords and different shades of khakis, held up by a weaved belt. I generally wore loafers, as a rule without socks. I was somewhat stout. I observed the principles. I was set out toward Yale.

Adam was the direct opposite of me. One, he was more seasoned than us all by two years. After middle school, his hipster guardians had hauled him out of school to work in a mission in one of the Salvadors, El or San. It should be one year, however it had transformed into two.

Two, he was brazenly liberal. His radicalism appeared in his style. He wore his dull hair long and free. He shaved just when constrained. He sat in the back. He tuned in to music in class. He pushed the edges of our clothing standard. He despised the line. After CODASCO, he was made a beeline for the College of the Atlantic in Bar Harbor, Maine, a trial school committed to the investigation of something many refer to as human nature.

Adam was likewise transparently gay. He didn't mind who knew. He was path relatively revolutionary.

Other than in show, our ways infrequently crossed. We unquestionably were not companions. We were well disposed uniquely in the manner that individuals are agreeable on the grounds that that is the thing that is anticipated from them. My folks abhorred impoliteness. They thought of it as low class.

I was neurotic when Adam requested that I read lines with him. I promptly presumed a ulterior intention. Probably the closest companion had the Ally Sheedy job, so she appeared to be a characteristic choice on the off chance that he required or needed to practice outside of practice.

Hereditarily unequipped for discourteousness, I concurred. In any case, I demanded we work some place public. I would not like to be the subject of insinuation and talk.

Insinuation and gossip twirled around Adam. Some guaranteed he went to the organic product circle in Forest Park for mysterious sex with more established men. Some asserted he and his closest companion growing up were beaus until they were gotten and the companion's folks constrained him to DeSmet for secondary school to move him away from Adam. Some guaranteed he would blow a person whenever asked, no assumptions and no hidden obligations. Nobody confessed to inquiring.

Everybody at school called me Jo, short for Mark (my dad was "Mark II" so I had everlastingly been "Jo" to his "Mark" to everybody in my family). I was shocked while, during our first time perusing together, Adam took it to a more private level and called me "JoJo." He brought down his jawline and limited his bruised eyes when he did.

"It would be ideal if you call me Jo or Mark," I said.

"No can do, JoJo," he replied, again bringing down his jaw and narrowing his eyes. "Jo's a young lady's name and Mark's are for prostitutes or for pissing and crapping. You're no young lady, and you're excessively lovely for piss or poo."

He was correct. I was pretty. I had brilliant blue eyes and enormously dim, long eyelashes. They looked phony and like I was wearing mascara. They were not and I was most certainly not.

Adam's grin was wily, practically wicked. His lips were full and brilliant red, and they normally remained together when he grinned. At the point when they didn't, his grin uncovered articulated canines and a left sidelong incisor that marginally covered with the focal incisor.

173

Adam was not equitably wonderful. Yet, he held himself with such certainty that he caused himself to appear to be more wonderful than he was. It was the certainty of somebody who knew what his identity was and what he was doing.

As we read lines, Adam put his hands on me a great deal. I jumped each time he went after me. "What's up, JoJo?" he inquired. "I don't chomp. . . . Except if, obviously, you need me to."

I had seen Adam like this with different young men. I didn't need it. "Stop it, Adam," I cautioned. "I will stop working with you. I will."

"You don't need me to stop. What's more, you know it."

He was correct. I don't have the foggiest idea how he knew it, since I didn't have any acquaintance with it. However, he was correct.

Following two or three weeks of working in homerooms and libraries, we migrated our practices to the second floor of my home, which I had all to myself. I don't recollect who originally recommended the migration, yet I realized it may predict something I didn't realize I needed.

I was filled with nervousness trusting that Adam will show up. I don't have the foggiest idea what compromised me more, the chance of activity or the chance of inaction.

Adam showed up straightforwardly from swimming training, in shorts and a tee, his wet hair tucked behind his ears. I acquainted him with my folks and, after a short trade, we higher up to my rooms to run lines. We went to my investigation and sat in work area seats, inverse one another.

As I read, Adam moved to the floor and began veering toward me. He snatched the legs of my seat and slid his legs through them. He was straightforwardly before me, his solid hands gradually manipulating my calves.

The bit of his hands tantalized and excited me. I was wearing just fighters and lattice shorts, and the impact he was having on me was self-evident.

"What are you doing?" I inquired.

"Just what you need," he said. "You're in control. At the point when you state stop, I'll stop."

I didn't utter a word. I returned to perusing lines as Adam's hands moved to my thighs. With each press, he went further up the leg of my shorts. I felt his thumbs where my thighs met my groin and afterward on my scrotum. I was stressing as he moved his correct hand to my glans, running his thumb in little circles around it. I could feel myself spilling. At the point when I peered down to see the proof, I saw wild desire in Adam's dim eyes. He took my hardness in his correct hand and began crushing and afterward gradually delivering it. He gazed at me as he did.

"Stand up," he at long last said.

I did, and he hauled my shorts out and afterward down. I was gazing down at him, my erection directly before his face. He gazed toward me, grinned, and inquired as to whether I was OK.

I was unable to reply. My mouth was so dry, I had gone quiet. I gestured here and there.

He kissed my glans, utilizing the tip of his tongue to hack up the thing I was spilling. I had never been in anybody's mouth, and I was enthusiastic for him to take me. Without deduction, I attempted to drive myself in.

He put his hands on my hips and said "Simple, JoJo, hinder a bit."

"I can't," I croaked.

He took my glans in his mouth, his tongue whirling around it the manner in which his thumb had. I figured I may drop. I again attempted to compel myself in, just to be opposed by his correct hand on my pelvis.

He took my balls in his left hand and took the length of me into his mouth. At the point when I was so profound he was breathing in my shrub, I felt the climax I needed to stifle crash however. I would not like to come, yet I was unable to forestall it. I filled his throat, humiliated by how little control I had appeared. He kept his mouth around me, and I felt him swallow whatever I had taken care of him before again feeling his tongue twirling around my glans and under my prepuce.

At the point when he was done, he gazed toward me, grinned, and again inquired as to whether I was alright. I actually couldn't reply. I was unable to accept what had occurred and didn't have the foggiest idea what was anticipated from me. I pulled my fighters and shorts up and sat down.

Adam moved back to his seat. He gazed at me as he pulled his shorts aside and began stroking himself.

"You can help, on the off chance that you need."

I needed, however I had no clue about what to do. Thus, I sat idle. I just watched him stir his hand here and there the shaft of his penis, which had all the earmarks of being more modest and more slender than mine.

Adam grinned at me as he jacked off. As he speeded up, I raised my eyes to his. He pulled his shirt up with his left hand, uncovering a tight path of dim hair from his navel into his shorts. He went ahead his stomach, quite a bit of pooling in his navel. He worked out every single drop that he could. He shook his head and shivered when he was done.
"Kindly make me something," he asked. He cleaned himself with the tissues with which I returned. At that point, he just sat and gazed at me, grinning comprehensively.

"That was my first time," I at long last stated, ending the quietness.

"Mine, as well," he replied. Suprised, I caused a commotion at him accordingly, and he immediately added "With a turtleneck."

"When was your genuine first time?"

"The previous summer. He was more seasoned. He trained me a great deal."

"Is it accurate to say that he was, similar to, your beau?"

"Kinda sorta. He was a companion of my brother's. We snuck around despite my sibling's good faith. He doesn't think about his companion."

"What occurred?"

"He returned to school."

I had 1,000,000 additional things to ask him. I had 1,000 comments to him. I did not one or the other.

"You should go," I said.

"OK," he stated, standing up and changing himself. Before he left, he kissed my temple and said "How about we get tomorrow where left off today."

As I jacked off that evening, the picture in my psyche was of Adam on his knees, my penis in his mouth. It was the first occasion when I had ever stroked off to picture of a person.

I was scared Adam would tell everybody. I strolled the corridors of CODASCO the following day trusting that somebody will inquire as to whether it was valid. Nobody did.

That night, Adam again showed up straightforwardly from swim practice. Dissimilar to the day preceding, there was no misrepresentation. When I shut the entryway to my examination room, he maneuvered me into him. I was extremely irresolute about kissing a kid, yet he was quietly tenacious. His mouth was firm and warm against mine, and my uncertainty immediately softened away. We kissed hard and long. As we did, he took me in his correct hand through my shorts and declared "I will suck you so hard" into my mouth.

He at that point continued to do precisely that, stooping before me and working his mouth to and fro on me as he moved his hands from my areolas to my sides and, at long last, to my hips. He moved me to and fro, constraining me to meet his slurping mouth. I kept going longer than I had the day preceding, yet just barely. At the point when I was done filling Adam's mouth, my legs were so unstable I needed to plunk down.

Adam slipped his shorts off and remained before me, his circumcised penis in my face. "Your turn."

I had never contacted a penis other than my own. I probably took it in my grasp, just to find his penis felt, all things considered, similar to my penis.

"Does it taste terrible?" I asked, gazing toward him.

"No. It tastes incredible."

I took him in my mouth. He didn't taste terrible, yet he likewise didn't taste incredible.

I had no clue about the thing I was doing. I think whatever I attempted wasn't right.

"Allow me to help," he said. I didn't know what he implied, until he set his left hand tenderly on the rear of my head and his correct hand around the base of his penis.

"Move your mouth with my hand."

I did, encouraged on by the hand in my hair. I was astounded by how simple it was once he demonstrated me what to do. I was additionally amazed by the sensation of control I had as I moved to and fro with his hand.

I felt him begin to annoy. I attempted to pull off, yet his left hand held me consistent as he came in my mouth. I gulped and choked. His cum was severe and sharp, yet I had no real option except to swallow a lot as he came a lot.

"Blech," I stated, when he was done. "That didn't taste great by any means."

"That is my shortcoming," he said. "We had asparagus with supper the previous evening. I ought to have skipped it."

"What you eat influences how it tastes?"

"It does. A great deal. I'll eat better around evening time."

The following day, I was hard before Adam shown up. I dreaded my folks would take note. I pulled on pressure shorts not long prior to going down to answer the entryway.

Adam was a dream. He had his dull hair pulled back in a braid. He had not shaved. He wore a dark tank, white shorts, and no shoes.

When he was through my investigation room entryway, I secured it and pulled him in me. "I need to make out for as long as possible," I recommended.

"Alright," he said. "Rests."

I did, on my bed, and he laid himself down on top of me. We were mouth to mouth, chest to chest, and groin to groin. We kissed constantly, our tongues battling and our groins crushing.

At the point when our mouths were crude, Adam offered that he "had a thought."

"What?"

"Take your shorts off, and I'll show you."

As I eliminated my shorts, Adam eliminated his. I felt inept with my shirt on, so I pulled it over my head. He did likewise. Unexpectedly, we were bare together.

Adam advised me to lie on my side, my legs twisted to uncover my groin. At the point when I did, he stuck to this same pattern, just inverse. It was evident what he needed, so I accepting him in my mouth as he took me in his. He put his correct hand around the base of my shaft and moved it in mood with his mouth. I did likewise to him, coordinating my musicality to his.

He halted long enough to propose that I "attempt to stand by until he does." It would require some exertion, as I suspected he probably had more control than I, a beginner to the entirety of this, did.

I considered anesthetic things like tasks and schoolwork to attempt to divert myself from what his hand and his mouth were doing to me. It worked momentarily, however not for long.

"Apologies, I stated, yet I can't keep down any more."

Adam met my declaration by grasping me hard and sucking me harder. I came more earnestly as yet, halting how I was doing him so I could ride the influx of my climax as far and as high as Possible.

"Fuck," I shouted, failing to remember my habits. "That was inconceivable."

"It was," he concurred. "Presently, return to work, and complete me."

I did as I was told, pivoting and bowing between his legs as I sucked him the customary way. At the point when I felt his hands in my hair, I grasped his scrotum with my left hand and worked his shaft with my correct hand and my mouth.

"Goodness God," he stated, as he raised his hips and came in my mouth. I constrained him back down, utilized my hands to squeeze his hips to the floor covering, and drained him dry with my mouth. After I gulped all he gave, I began to snicker.

"For what reason are you giggling?" He inquired.

"You were correct. That tasted much better."

"That's right. No asparagus the previous evening. Pineapple squeeze today."

We went on like that, running lines and trading sensual caresses. At the point when the play was finished, Adam and JoJo were most certainly not. He continued coming over, and we kept at one another. Adam was a cocksucker, in the most genuine feeling of the word. He adored doing it, and it appeared in how great he was grinding away. I kidded that it was no mishap his initials were CS, as though his name had predetermined his ability.

"What would i be able to state?" he derided back. "I'm a pig for dick."

He was. He blew me again and again and over, way more as often as possible than I blew him.

At school, I held my ear to the ground. I didn't hear anything. Adam was genuinely prudent, and we were wary. We claimed not to know one another, consistently.

He violated at graduation. After he had gathered his recognition, he grabbed my attention as he got back to his seat. At the point when he did, he winked at me. I jumped. I shut my eyes, certain all the world had seen that wink, that the earth had quit turning, and that when I opened my eyes I would be at the focal point of the glare.

I was definitely not. At the point when I opened my eyes, graduates proceeded to walk, and guardians kept on acclaiming. My graduation neighbors kept on remembering me for their disrespectful chitchat.

CODACO's graduation celebration is an all-graduate occasion. I ran into Adam as I worked my way around. He was staggering in an untucked white shirt, dull pants, and no shoes. He shook my hand and said "Congrats, JoJo." As usual, he brought down his jawline and said "JoJo" fiendishly.

"As far as you might be concerned, as well, Adam."

He moved his mouth to my ear and murmured delicately. "I thought maybe we could celebrate secretly later. . . . Would i be able to remain with you this evening?"

I didn't have a clue how to reply. Some portion of me was apprehensive, as what he proposed appeared to be another level, one for which I didn't know, in the clamor of the gathering, I was prepared. The other piece of me needed to get his wrist and escape with him at that point.

"I didn't have any acquaintance with both of you knew one another," intruded on Jennifer, a schoolmate I had been chipping away at for as long as couple of weeks and with whom I thought I was going to settle the negotiation. I had swore to lose my virginity before I left for school, and I had recognized Jennifer as the destined to help me keep my promise. We had been closest companions since kindergarten. Her birthday was the exact day as mine, and that incident had appeared at five years of age to be the ideal motivation to be closest companions. Our kinship had suffered since.

"We ran lines together for the play," I contributed, rapidly.

"Indeed," Adam added. "I was battling. Jo benevolently offered to help me."

187

"Indeed, it worked," Jennifer added. "You were awesome."

"Much obliged to you," Adam replied, winking at me and walking off.

She was correct. I had been acceptable, yet Adam had been incredible. He was gifted in a manner I was definitely not.

Soon thereafter, I got Adam alone, outside. He had his keys out and appeared as though he was prepared to leave. He gave his keys a snappy clank and grinned at me.

"I'll be hanging tight for you," he said.

Desire penetrated me. I was unable to stand by. I hauled Adam behind a tree and squeezed my lips to his.

"Jo?" I heard Jennifer call out. Instinctually, I drove Adam away.

Uncertain of what she had seen, I yelped "Get off me, Faggot."

"What's happening?" Jennifer asked, coming around the tree.

"He hauled me behind the tree and attempted to kiss me," I stated, hustling to her side. "I advised him to get off me." I was debilitated as I lied.

As we left, I thought back to Adam. He was gazing derisively at me, shaking his head to and fro disgustedly. My stomach tied, as I saw no benevolence in his face.

I lost my virginity to Jennifer that evening. As I slid all through her, I envisioned she was Adam. We had never done that, and my disloyalty implied we never would.
I called Adam when I woke up the following morning. Nobody replied.

I called over and again for the duration of the day. His mom at last replied around five, asked what it's identity was, and afterward demanded Adam was not at home. I left a directive for him to call me. He didn't.

I laid down with Jennifer again that evening, taking her from behind. She was warm and wet and smooth inside.

She had attempted to give me a sensual caress, yet she was horrendous at it. I needed to guide her, yet I was concerned she would consider how I knew. Thus, I pulled her up, turned her around, and imagined she was Adam.

I got a similar dance and melody from Adam's mom the following day.

I spent the following week sustaining a similar daily schedule. I imagined Jennifer was Adam as I conveyed myself to her. Also, at that point I imagined Adam was not keeping away from me when I attempted to find him, similar to my disloyalty of him had not constrained an irreversible break.

After a couple of all the more apathetic endeavors, I surrendered. Adam had ghosted me. I merited it. I had secured myself. In this manner, I had lost some of what I was ensuring.

I never got with or saw Adam again. I covered my torment and myself in Jennifer the remainder of the late spring. I screwed her as regularly as Possible to demonstrate to myself that I was straight. I pledged to leave the Adam Interregunum behind me.

Chapter Two

At Yale, I proposed to proceed on the tight and straight way I had set with Jennifer. I immediately discovered that the way to hellfire is cleared with honest goals.

A principled traditionalist, I joined the Tory Party in the Yale Political Union. Albeit just a green bean, I sparkled as a debater. At CODASCO, I had retained books by William Buckley, Edmund Burke, Ayn Rand, and each other moderate mastermind. I was knowledgeable in moderate political hypothesis and thought.

As I went to an ever increasing number of discussions, I really wanted to see "Thatcher" Rees, a Junior who was additionally in my school. Despite the fact that his name was Edward, he demanded "Thatcher" to respect Margaret Thatcher, his courageous woman. "Cover" was a Tory completely. He was from Choate, and he was interested by my appearance from the Midwest.

"Cover" was more special than I was. He had experienced childhood in the Racquet Club of Philadelphia. He was a cultivated squash player. He cruised. He shunned conventional American games like baseball and football as "normal."

He was an athletic, not built, 6'4". His wavy earthy colored hair was great. His thick earthy colored eyebrows were awesome. His dark eyes were great. His catch nose was great. His straight, white teeth were great. His etched, solid jaw was awesome. His word usage was great. He articulated the "h" in "where" and the "th" in "garments." He said each word precisely as it was proposed to be said. He seemed as though I envisioned James Bond had looked, when he was youthful and administering a grounds. He looked like Jude Law in The Talented Mr. Ripley, just with more obscure hair.

Gradually, I was distraught for him in a way I had never been for any other individual. I fixated on him. I hurt when we were not together.

From numerous points of view, I needed to be him. I needed to walk the lobbies that he strolled, deserve the fondness and admiration that he told, and arrogate his part to myself when he left Yale.

Be that as it may, I additionally needed to be with him. Adam had whetted a craving that Jennifer and the young ladies through whom I worked my way at Yale couldn't satisfy.

We got indistinguishable and private in a thoughtful manner. We were loving in a dispassionate manner. I looked and hung tight for even the trace of something else. I never discovered it. On the off chance that Thatch had even the smallest interest in same sex, he never sold out it to me.

We lived respectively his last year and my second. I ought to have known better. The vicinity just sparked my interest. I saw a lot of him. I saw his wide shoulders, his stuffed stomach, his solid legs, and his adjusted ass. I saw him trickling wet after the shower, his chest hair smooth to his chest. I saw him ricochet in and tent his fighters. I saw him slip into his pressure shorts, his penis supported against his scrotum as he pulled them up. I saw him lay his hand on his lump as he leaned back and read in his bed.

I likewise heard excessively. He nitty gritty his sexploits to me. He was a kiss and tell. He screwed a ton of young ladies, and he jumped at the chance to inform me concerning them when he got back to our room

"Mark, awaken," he would state. "You're not going to accept this one."

I'd move toward him, and he would reveal to me how he had coaxed a young lady to accomplish something she had swore she never would, regardless of whether it was letting him cum all over, allowing him to screw her in the ass, or something in the middle. I'd get as hard as a stone tuning in to him.

He took sex back to our room just when he needed to. At the point when he called my name, I needed to imagine I was snoozing. I would tune in to young ladies heave and gasp under him. I never saw him hard, however the responses of the young ladies proposed he was either enriched or realized how to fuck or both. I regularly considered what it resembles to be them, to feel the heaviness of him on top of me, to feel his dick enter and afterward spread me, the fill him let completely go and fill me. I fantasized about losing my equivalent sex virginity to Thatcher.

Not long prior to Spring break, I flipped everything completely around. We were tanked and high and chuckling on his bed. I put my head on his shoulder, and he put his head against my head. I began stimulating the highest point of his lower arm.

"What are you doing, Mark?" he asked, yet not at all that frightened me. It appeared to be more guiltless than disturbing.

I turned my face to his voice, and he grinned at me. I mixed up his grin as a greeting, and I pushed my mouth toward his. He yanked his head back, pummeling it against the divider.

He hopped off the bed furiously. "What the hell, Mark?"

I froze. "I don't have the foggiest idea why I did that. I'm tanked and high."

"I'm not a fag!"

"I'm not all things considered. . . . If you don't mind please it would be ideal if you Thatch, don't be distraught and don't tell anybody. It was a slip-up. It isn't who I am. I don't have the foggiest idea what came over me. I was being inept. I was playing a game."

It was clear he didn't trust me my conflicting, froze claims. He saw me like I was a more unusual he had never met and had no interest in knowing. He followed out of the room, pummeling the entryway hard behind him.

I was shaking, attempting to sort out some way to deflect the looming emergency. I began believing that I would need to move and pondering where I could or would go. I nodded off, plotting.

Cover went back and forth as I dozed. I saw little of him before break. Things were totally extraordinary between us the remainder of the year. We infrequently were together. At the point when we were, he scarcely addressed me. He was not straightforwardly antagonistic, but rather he was an outsider. He turned out well for him, and I went mine.

I left a graduation present for him, alongside a note saying 'sorry' for losing my head. He never recognized possibly one.

As should have been obvious, he never advised anybody I had attempted to kiss him. Yet, I had destroyed a companionship and taken in an exercise I could always remember.

*****

I requested Vivian out the main day from my Junior year. I had since quite a while ago known about her, however her school was a long way from mine, and we had experienced each other just in passing during our initial two years in New Haven.

That day, I was behind her in line at the Union, so I presented myself. "I know what your identity is," she said. "Everybody knows what your identity is."

"Truly?" I inquired. "I didn't realize I was known."

"You are. You are the lone Tory we as a whole need to save, particularly since Thatcher is no more."

"You should attempt. You can begin once again supper."

We had an incredible first date that finished with the guarantee of something else. We engaged in sexual relations after our

196

subsequent date. At the point when we were done, she offered "I surmise that responds to that."

"Answers what?" I inquired.

"A few of us contemplated whether you were gay. In reality, we thought perhaps you and Thatcher were gay together. Both of you appeared to be a couple. At that point, both of you appeared to be a couple who had separated."

"We were definitely not. We were companions who had a spat over something little that we let get large until it was too huge to be little once more. It was inept."

To demonstrate to her I was not gay, I went down on her until she shouted out. At that point, I stuck her legs to her shoulders and screwed her once more, as enthusiastically as Possible. It was the first occasion when I had ever engaged in sexual relations without a condom on. I had wanted to pull out when I drew near to decrease the danger as much as could be expected under the circumstances, yet I didn't. Her velvet felt excessively great. Indeed, even as she said "no" I covered myself within her as profoundly as Possible and filled her.

At the point when I understood what I had done, I froze. "Gracious my God, I am so grieved. I ought not have done that."

"It's fine," she said. "We simply must be more cautious next time."

We were. We held up until she got a stomach. After not wearing one once, I never needed to wear a condom again. What's more, she detested the pill.

Whenever we were ensured, we had as much sex as possible. I was attempting to demonstrate something to myself.

We turned into the most conspicuous couple nearby. We strolled here and far off inseparably. Vi was brought up in tip top groups of friends, and she kept on running in them. Her companions turned into my companions.

Our sexual coexistence was dynamic, however atavistic. Vi enjoyed sex, however she was not audacious about it. She liked to be on her back, her legs level. She would not permit me to take her from behind, declaring it was base and brutal. She permitted me to contact her bosoms and her body, however she scarcely gave back in kind. Her hands seldom wandered over me. Her tongue never did. On the off chance that she contacted my dick, it was uniquely to direct me back within her. She permitted me to go down on her, yet she stayed away forever the kindness. She didn't care for fellatio. She loathed cum.

It was unfulfilling. I jumped at the chance to be contacted. I loved the glow of a hand on my shoulder, the palm of a hand on my chest, the suggestion of a tongue winding down my sides and made a beeline for my groin. I needed forplay to be shared. Our own was definitely not. Vi was a beneficiary, not a member.

*****

Albeit Vi and I were dug in as a couple, I needed to effectively battle to stifle the base urges that snuck just underneath my surface. They state "a large portion of the fight is the will to take up arms." My will was solid, and I braced it by evading circumstances where I may be enticed. I invested as much energy with Vi as possible. I maintained a strategic distance from personal fellowships with young men. I dodged any kid to whom I ended up pulled in.

When Luther Gordon showed up nearby, I had not been with a man for over three years. I had gained from my misfortune with Thatcher, and I sublimated any fascination I needed to anybody other than Vi.

I was beginning my Senior year, and Luther was a Junior exchange who was to be the point watch on Yale's woeful b-ball group. At that point, Yale had not been to the NCAA Tournament since 1962. Until this year, it actually had not.

Lute's appearance was exceptionally envisioned. He should be a fantastic watchman. He was likewise expected to be a virtuoso and flawless.

Lute was as proclaimed. Thinking nothing about ball other than that it exhausted me to tears, I was unable to assess his athletic abilities. However, the individuals who thought often about such things anticipated that him should change Yale into an Ivy League competitor. He was depicted as an astounding ball controller and as having a stroke so sweet he was recognized as a "unadulterated shooter." I laughed about how sexual b-ball appeared.

I could assess his mind. Shockingly, he turned into the principal dark individual from the Tory Club and quickly turned into an amazing powerhouse. He had all the contentions down. He appeared to have perused all that I had perused. He was persuasive and learned such that made me all around envious.

I could likewise assess his looks. He was dazzling. He had a straightforward, untroubled face. His eyes were huge and "doey." His nose was little and thrashed. His lips were thick and shapely. His teeth were huge and straight and white. They made his grin, which was wide and dissolved margarine. His face was stubbled. At the point when I later saw William DeMerritt in The Outs, I was shipped back to Yale and Lute.

His body overshadowed his face. Each of the 76 crawls of him gave off an impression of being etched from rock. His garments appeared to adhere to his skin. I had never been pulled in to an individual of color previously, however I was unable to keep my eyes off of "Lute." Almost every time he took a gander at me, I was at that point taking a gander at him. I would rapidly deflect my eyes, however I realized he was timing me.

I additionally realized I was burning through my time. As I heard it, Lute was riding his way through grounds as fast as possible, leaving broken young ladies - every one of them white - afterward, requiring and needing more than he was eager to give.

We were both at a similar gathering not long before the beginning of Fall break. I was all alone, as Vi had made a beeline for D.C. for the long end of the week.

I made an effort not to follow him with my eyes, yet I bombed pitiably. I realized he was seeing me notice him, however I was unable to prevent myself from seeing him.

Before I got excessively enticed to plot, I said my farewells and made a beeline for Silliman. I was suprised to hear a "Jo, hold up" as I did. I realized it was Lute pursuing me down.

"Where are you going at the present time?" he inquired.

"Simply back to my room."

"Accompany me all things considered."

I did, following him past Silliman to Dwight. As opposed to going to the rooms, we headed ground floor and down a long corridor.

"Where are we going?" I inquired.

"You'll see."

After one turn, he opened an entryway, guided me into a little room that was more similar to a storeroom, and pulled the entryway shut behind us, locking it. It was a burial chamber until he flicked on a little light. At the point when my eyes changed, I saw that we were, indeed, in a changed over brush wardrobe that was populated with two bean sacks, covers, a little table, and a little cooler.

"What is this?"

"Two or three us set it up. We consider it The Hole. We descend here when we need harmony or protection or when we need to get high."

"What are we doing here?" I asked, underlining the we.

"I figured we may require some protection."

"For what?" I asked, not in any way expecting what returned at me.

"To sort out why you watch me to such an extent."

I needed to jolt. I dreaded he had timed me and had carried me to The Hole to menace or beat me.

I chose the best protection was a decent offense. "You watch me as much as I watch you. Perhaps you should sort out why you do that."

"I don't need to," he said. "I definitely know."

"Why do you do it?" I asked, my throat choking with dread.

He moved straightforwardly before me. I prepared myself for what I dreaded was coming.

I misread him totally. Instead of drill his finger into my chest or punch me in the stomach, he put his correct hand on my shoulder and, in the gentlest voice I had ever heard, stated, "I was attempting to sort out what you'd do . . . on the off chance that I did this." He at that point brought his mouth down to mine and sent a blue fire down my throat, through my crotch, and out through my toes. I addressed him silently, opening my mouth and permitting his tongue the opportunity to go crazy inside. His lips were firm and full. His grasp was tight. His tongue was forceful and huge and solid. He was amazing in a manner Adam had not been.

When I got my ocean legs, I kissed him back as hard as he was kissing me. I battled his tongue with my own. Two inches more limited than his 6'4", I needed to pull his head to all mine the kiss unblemished.

He slid his hands down my back, grasped my rear, and constrained his hips into mine. An unrecognizable commotion sputtered out of my chest.

At the point when the kiss at last finished, I wheezed for air. As I did, Lute looked at me straightforwardly without flinching, moved his hands to my belt and zipper, and argued "I need to screw you, Jo" before he began kissing me once more.

I held. I got his hands and pulled my mouth from his. "I have never done that," I conceded through worn out breaths.

"There's a first an ideal opportunity for everything," he guaranteed me, pulling his hands liberated from mine and pulling my shirt up. I had no real option except to raise my arms and permit him to take off my shirt totally. He tossed it to the floor and pulled my body toward him, bringing his mouth down to my correct areola as his hands again worked my belt and my zipper.

As he battled to liberate me, I dominated, opening my khakis and pulling them and my fighters down. It had been quite a while since Adam, and my stifled, base cravings broke free.

Lute utilized my independence for his potential benefit, pulling his shirt over his head, uncovering a solid chest with a thick fix of wavy hair directly in the center. He at that point opened and ventured out of his khakis, uncovering thick legs likewise covered with wavy hair. At the point when he pulled his fighters down and off, we were exposed with one another.

I was hard, my whole penis calling attention to straight and bended somewhat upward. Lute was likewise hard, his cut and proportionate penis longer and thicker than mine. It, as well, stood straight out and was marginally bended upward.

I had no clue about what to do. I admitted my reserve. "I have just given a few penis massages, and I don't think they were excellent," I conceded.

"We will go on a decent outing together," he guaranteed me, bringing me into his hand. "I like that you're whole," he said. "It's a pleasant difference in speed."

He moved before me, held us both in his enormous right hand, and began to stroke us together as he kissed my mouth once more. "Don't you dare come," he murmured into my mouth.

"Before long, I will have no way out."

"At that point how about we move to better things," he stated, bringing his mouth down to my neck and licking his way down my body to my groin. He held my hips as he took me right to the base. I was hypnotized watching my white penis slide all through his earthy colored face and his thick, delicate lips. I began to come. I was unable to help it. It had been excessively long.

Luke didn't mind that I came without notice him. He gulped and continued onward, depleting all I advertised.

At the point when he was done, he requested me to stoop more than one of the bean packs. I was scared by what he expected to do.

Lute was capable, and he licked and extended me with his finger until he thought I was prepared. I was frightened, yet I was additionally provoked up by the lashing he had given my opening.

He sheathed himself and squeezed at me from behind. Amazingly, I needed him within me, similar to I had never needed anything.

"You need to unwind," he murmured in my ear. "I'm not going to hurt you."

I breathed out profoundly and felt him begin me. "Better believe it, much the same as that," he said. "Open to me. Give me access."

I breathed out profoundly again as I felt Lute work himself in. "OK," he said. "My head is right in. The crucial step's finished. Presently, simply relax. Furthermore, unwind."

He worked himself to and fro gradually, moving in somewhat more profound with each push ahead. He continued murmuring "inhale" and "no doubt, much the same as that" in my ear as he did. His hot breath in my ear was sensual as heck, and it eclipsed the distress of opening to him.

"I'm right in," he murmured. "I'm simply going to hold here and allowed you to change in accordance with me. Take full breaths and attempt to unwind as much as could be expected under the circumstances."

I did as he trained. With each breath, I felt increasingly more of the dread die down.

"Are you prepared for me to screw you, white kid?" he inquired. I was. Extremely prepared. I gestured my head, and he began to move all through me, gradually and without a doubt.
"Goodness my God," I said.

"Goodness my God is correct," he replied.

Utilizing his hands, he constrained my face and shoulders into the bean pack. I moved my hands to my face and held it.

"Goodness, fuck, I will come," I got with behind me. "I will come in your tight white ass."

He slammed into me so hard I figured I would tear. Over and over. I could tell he was coming. I whimpered as he did, somewhat out of torment, and halfway out of delight.

"Shhh" he murmured as he pulled out of me, eliminated the condom, tied it, and dropped it in a Ziplock sack. "Disguising the proof" he stated, dropping the sack on the floor to be taken with us and discarded later.

He at that point implored me to respond. I was stunned getting screwed was something any person needed, as opposed to something he was happy to suffer as a component of a fallen angel's deal.

He had me take him from the front. He was on his back on a bean sack, his legs high and wide as he guided me toward him. I was suprised by how effectively I entered him. He shut his eyes, turned his head aside, and permitted me to screw him as I needed. I endured longer than I anticipated, likely a side-effect of being blown so as of late. As he asked me on, I began to perspire and afterward I came so hard I was sure I had burst the condom. I had not. It, as well, went into the ziplock pack and afterward with us when we left.

Nothing I had done before contrasted with what I had quite recently done. I had adored screwing and being screwed by Lute, and I certainly needed to do it once more.

Chapter Three

We met in The Hole the following night at 10. We didn't imagine our gathering was for any reason other than the undeniable one. We began stripping when we bolted the entryway behind us. We kissed momentarily before he bowed me over and took me from behind once more.

At the point when he was done, he advised me to screw him against the entryway, at that point turned his back to me. I moved on a condom, gotten his hips, and squeezed into him. I kissed the delicate skin in his back. He smelled not the same as any man I had ever smelled.

I ran my hands over his lats and his shoulders as I gradually moved all through him. I stretched around him, he took my hands in his, and he held them to his chest as he moved against me. When I came, he was level against the entryway, which was hitting musically against the jam with us. Bang, pound, pound.

At the point when I was done, we subsided into the bean sacks, he lit a joint and we, unexpectedly, talked. "I thought you were a pussy dog," I advertised.

"I thought you had a sweetheart."

"I do have a sweetheart."

"Furthermore, I am a pussy dog."

"At that point what is this?"

"Nothing more needs to be said. I like the two sides of the seesaw."

"I don't know that I do," I replied, less convincingly than I had trusted.

"You appear to, particularly when you're covered within me. Or on the other hand, when I'm covered within you and you're beseeching me for more than I must give."

I reddened brilliant red. I had trusted he had not heard me murmur "further" as he screwed me.

Lute came to over and clasped my hand with his. "I'm simply busting you," he stated, lifting my hand to his mouth and licking its rear.

He offered me a portion of his joint. I declined. "Pot makes me horny."

"At that point have a few."

"I needn't bother with it," I replied, more fair than I had proposed to be.

"Show me."

I moved between his legs and began running my hands once again his hard, ripped chest and stomach. His skin was gentler than any skin I had ever contacted.

He developed as I moved my hands to his thighs. I tongued his balls and where his legs met his groin. I didn't care for the bristly hair against my face. In any case, I enjoyed his penis, a ton. It was smooth, not veiny, and thick with a dull, practically purple, head.

I took him in my mouth and began to stroke him. I felt him move to his feet as I did. He snatched the hair on the highest point of my head and began sliding himself all through my mouth. "Take that dick," I heard him state. "Suck my large dark dick."

I was astounded that his way and his words turned me on. Yet, they did. I loved that he was in control and requesting. I loved being constrained.

I had him in an oral bad habit. I crushed his balls as he kept choking my face. I felt his climax start in my grasp and move past my lips and into my throat, hot and thick. "Fuck" was all I heard as he clasped, his dick jumping out of my mouth. I gulped and sat back on my rump, sweat-soaked and tired. I chuckled discreetly to myself.

"What are you chuckling at?" he asked, finishing his inquiry with a relational word.

"I figured your cum may taste unique."

"Diverse how?"

"I don't have the foggiest idea. Chocolatey, possibly."

"You're a damn numb-skull, Mark. Does a white kid's cum taste like vanilla?"

"No. Furthermore, I know better. I just idea perhaps. All things considered, I trusted perhaps. I'm not a devotee of that taste."

"Become one. You need to swallow mine without fail. It's inconsiderate not to. In case I will allow you to suck my dick, you need to do it right."

"No doubt about it?"

"Definitely your white ass I am," he said. "Furthermore, presently, I will allow you to screw me."

He pushed me in reverse into a bean sack and began to bring down himself onto me.

"Hang on," I said. "I'm not wearing a condom."

"I couldn't care less," he said. "I need this . . . at this moment," he stated, as he filled his hand with spit with which he at that point covered me.

His chest was in my face as he rode me. Now and then, he would stand, removing from me and placing his dick in my mouth. As I got him close with my mouth, he would pull out, and lower himself back onto me. We went to and fro like that until I was unable to last any more and I came. I cycle his chest. He maneuvered my head into his chest as hard as possible. I continued gnawing as he did. He came not long after I did, directly into the center of my chest.

We went on like that the remainder of the semester. During the day, Vi and I walked inseparably through Cross Campus and Old Campus, Yale's "Dynamic Duo," the image of flawlessness. Vi was a wonderful, keen lady, free and solid. I was an attractive, shrewd man, advantaged and made a beeline for more advantage.

During the evening, I took away to meet Lute at whatever point I could. A few evenings, I went from Vi's bed to The Hole, wanting to discover Lute hanging tight for me. Different evenings, Lute and I plotted to meet at 2 a.m., when the grounds was snoozing.

Lute and I were not darlings. We were not even companions. We scarcely talked. We shut the entryway behind us, bolted it, and go to work. We were simply satisfying a need. Lute joyfully got things done to my body that I required and needed that Vi would not. Some of them - a hand on my chest or side, a tongue on my areola - were basic. Others - gulping my penis and my cum, licking my rear-end, sucking my toes - were definitely not.

I did likewise for him, satiating necessities and needs he had that his ladies would not endeavor to fulfill. He cherished having his balls licked and sucked. He preferred ass play, including a covered finger when he was going to come in my mouth. He enjoyed having his armpits licked.

Like me, Lute demanded what we were doing had no extraordinary importance. We were only two young men, getting off.

"See, Jo, I've been with a couple of folks. However, I've been with far more young ladies. I like young ladies and will totally will end up with a young lady. I'm simply playing with folks. What's more, playing with a person doesn't mean you're gay or you won't wind up with a young lady."

His conviction and his words impacted me. As far as I might be concerned, there was a gorge between how I was doing him and what my identity was. Vi - or somebody like Vi - was my future. Lute was an energizing recess, however I was persuaded he didn't be anything more than that.

*****

B-ball made my last semester additionally testing. Lute was gone a great deal. I worried about what and who he was doing when he was no more.

I was schocked when Lute revealed to me he needed to watch me screw Vi. We had quite recently screwed, meeting late in the red after the group's transport got back from Ithaca.

"Why?"

"I'm a voyeur. I like pornography, particularly genuine pornography."

I don't have the foggiest idea why, however I consented to set it up. Lute was in my storeroom, and I was conscious of his solicitations: go down on her, make her come, screw her evangelist style, no covers, pull out, ride her, please her tits.

It was simpler to pull off than I anticipated. Furthermore, realizing Lute was in my storage room viewing turned me totally on. Until this point, it was the best sex Vi and I had ever had. When I made her accompany my mouth, she gave totally in. She didn't act irritated when I dumped everywhere on her tits.

"That was hot," Lute revealed to me later, strapped. "In any case, white people and dark people don't screw the same by any means."

"In what capacity?" I inquired.

"All things considered, you screwed her as you didn't need no one to realize you were screwing. At the point when I screw a young lady, I screw her like I need everybody to realize she's getting screwed, and like I need her to recall what it resembled to get screwed by me."

He offered to show me, and I took him up on an it. A couple of evenings later, I was in his storeroom while he screwed a white young lady into blankness. He overwhelmed her, nailing her down, and pushing her around. When he entered her, she was beseeching him for it.

"Beseech me to screw you," he requested.

"If you don't mind screw me, I'm beseeching you," she replied.

As he screwed her, the bed shook. Lute was verbal, requesting that she disclose to him the amount she adored it, how large he was, and how much joy his enormous dark cockerel was bringing her. It was exciting, yet in addition upsetting. It verged

218

on sexism, however she didn't appear to take note. She had her legs as wide as she could get them and was winded when Lute declared he planned to come, pulled out, and dumped everywhere all over.

"Reveal to me you love my cum," he requested.

"I love your cum," she conceded, agreeably.

"Wipe it off your face and eat it."

She did. She flinched with the primary swallow, however he demanded she "eat everything."

Later in the red, I admitted to Lute that I had been both excited and disturbed by what I had seen. "Look," he said. "I'm an individual of color. White people have been pushing me around and guiding me my entire life. Indeed, even on the b-ball court. I have never been trained by an individual of color. In the room, I will push white people around and guide them. I'm in control. I make the standards. It's a tsicar represent me."

"Tsicar?" I inquired.

"It's 'bigot' in reverse. It's converse bigot. It's the retribution of the individual of color. That is the reason I just screw white young ladies and white young men. Like you."

I didn't realize whether to respect or detest him. I picked not one or the other. I just continued screwing him.

*****

The prior night graduation, Lute and I remained strapped. Long after we ought to have been spent, we continued ricocheting back for "once again." We realized we were sharing our last time together. I was leaving New Haven the following day for Chicago with Vi. Lute was remaining behind to continue playing ball, to continue discussing, and to continue to contemplate. Our run had been sensual and extraordinary and licentious, yet it was fleeting. It couldn't and would not last. It was a fume.

The morning of graduation, Lute stooped before me and gave me my graduation blessing. At the point when he was done, I gave back in kind with my farewell blessing.

As I dressed for the function; I didn't perceived myself. There was a gap between the individual I thought I was and the individual I really was. I was unable to perceive what Vi saw or what my folks saw. I could scarcely stand what I saw.

After the service was finished, I went to Chicago with Vi. I pledged to leave Lute and Adam and all that garbage in my rearview reflect, the interval over, my curiousity controlled. I promised that I had screwed and sucked my last person.

Chapter Four

For the initial two years Vi and I were in Chicago, I maintained my promise. My will was solid, and I was an extremely focused man.

Vi and I remained the "Dynamic Duo." My cohorts begrudged us.

There was likewise a staggering triviality to us. There was no there. We were all over, yet not profound. I knew it, however I required Vi to support me, to fortify my will.

As I composed before, my will disintegrated when I saw Mace in Bryan Cave's library. I caused a commotion and my hand to him as I cruised by. He grinned back, his cheeks coordinating the dimples on his jawline. I knew without further ado I was lost. I didn't have the foggiest idea thus couldn't clarify how or why, yet I was more overpowered by him than I had been by anybody, including Thatcher.

I made a special effort to request him. I visited his office. I welcomed him out.

He was either detached or modest, I didn't know which. He was hard to get into. I needed to drive his considerations out of him, and when I did, they turned out in drabs and dribs. Yet, for being overpowered by him, I would have deserted him, the push to separate him to an extreme.

I likewise pondered about him. He routinely floated away. He would be locked in and connecting and afterward meander away intellectually, present yet not there.

I dedicated him "the Carrot." I welcomed him for a Friday night out.

We changed at my loft. Mace was living with his folks in St. Charles, which was probably the dreariest thing I could envision. One, it was a brief drive every route through substantial traffic. Two, St. Charles is for the most part low end. Three, Mace had grown up poor, and I envisioned his folks were all the while living that way.

Mace shocked me when he played Yaz's "Mr. Blue." It appeared to be portentous that we shared that melody.

222

I empowered Mace rest over. He truly had no way out. He was in no shape to head to St. Charles.

He was almost sleeping on the lounge chair when I prodded him toward my bed. "This won't do," I said. "It will be too splendid come morning. Stay with me. There is a lot of room."

He followed me to my room. He didn't have any acquaintance with it, yet we were on our way.

The following morning, I got some information about himself. I was disheartened and shocked when he informed me regarding the demise of his more youthful sister, just a year prior in a fender bender. At the point when he completed, he was crying. I maneuvered him into me.

"I'm upset for bringing her up," I said. "In any case, I am happy to know. It clarifies a ton."

He caused a commotion, quietly asking "what?"

"There is a going thing on behind your eyes more often than not. In any event, when you are living it up, there is something keeping you down, prowling. What's more, you get lost a great deal."

"Lost?"

"Truly. It resembles you float away. You are there, yet you are definitely not."

*****

Mace moved in. Regrettably, he moved a bed with his garments. We had been sharing my bed, which I expected would proceed. His bed was a mishap I had not envisioned.

We talked space to room. It was feasible, however I utilized the clumsiness to determine the mishap. I proposed he should simply remain with me, similar to he had. He concurred. It had not taken a lot to acquire his arrangement. I had not needed to wheedle him.

I didn't advise him; however I was stripped that first night he rejoined me. I generally dozed bare. I had not with him already. I would going ahead.

The following evening, I demanded he get stripped, as well. It was a remarkable second. In the event that he opposed, my target might be postponed or even denied.

He didn't help it. We stayed on our way.

I raised the subject of same sex. Not at all like Thatch, Mace didn't redirect me. He bounced directly in, concurring with my hypothesis that a man would almost certainly be greater at pleasuring another man than a lady was. We were made a beeline for one another.

The cushion was taken out.

The sheet fell.

Our dicks contacted. We went ahead one another. Mace's dick was fantastic, long and thick and totally formed. It overshadowed mine. Also, any that I had ever seen.

Vi visited. I considered Mace I screwed her. I was unable to hold back to screw him.

I likewise couldn't trust that Vi will leave. I required and needed to be sleeping with Mace. I required and needed to put my lips to his. I required and needed to follow his collar bone, his chest, his hip bone. I required and needed to feel him, to satisfy him, to contact him, to cherish him.

I took him in my grasp. He took me in his.

I lied about never having been with a man. Mace accepted my untruth. I felt misleading, yet I likewise felt that he would withdraw on the off chance that he realized I had been plotting from the start.

Our mouths contacted.

I urgently needed my mouth on Mace's dick. I stood up to. I was driving the vehicle, yet I required Mace to think he was. I needed to hang tight for him.

As I trusted, he hopped first. His mouth on my dick was the most perfect delight I had ever felt. My desire was gone, supplanted by a standing, profound love that overshadowed totally anything I had ever felt for Thatch. I realized I was infatuated with Mace. I took off at seeing him.

Lightning had struck. We had gotten it in a container. We set the limit for tight. We could never allow it to out.

Chapter Five

Mace was so steadfast and solid. He needed us, unmistakably and without reservation.

I felt carefree close to him. I needed us, as well, however not completely. I needed us as a side dish, not as a course.

In my psyche, I would wed, Mace would wed, our kids would play together, our spouses would get to know one another, and they would discuss whatever ladies talk about while Mace and I sucked and screwed and lived and cherished behind their backs. Mace was too brilliant to even consider thinking my messed up variant of the fantasy might work out as expected.

At the point when I was with Mace, I was completely alive. I had begun needing to possess him. However, he claimed me, body and soul.

We were simply getting into the swing of us when it was the ideal opportunity for Mace to go to New York to see Ellie. I didn't know how sure he was about where we were, and I worried that a few days of Ellie would help Mace to remember what he had been. I jumped.

"Try not to go to New York this end of the week, Carrot. Stay here with me."

He cannot. However, he slid down my stomach and took the tip of me in his mouth. I jumped at his touch. In any case, I recovered my certainty that an end of the week with Ellie would not be the finish of Mark and Mace.

The following morning, I asked Mace when he originally pondered about me.

"Honestly?"

"Obviously."

"Heading to Blueberry Hill. You chimed in to Vogue. Straight men don't chime in to Vogue."

"I'm straight, Carrot," I said. "This isn't a thing; it is simply you." I needed Mace to feel unique. Furthermore, I needed Mace to be agreeable in the thing we were doing.

Mace asked me a similar inquiry.

"You kept me speculating. I thought perhaps first thing. However, at that point there was Ellie, your sense to rest on the lounge chair, and your nature to re-visitation of your bed. At the point when you slipped your briefs off with just a bit of inciting, I thought 'oh goodness, here we go.'"

"Was that the arrangement?" he asked, calling me out. I let a trace of trustworthiness spill out.

"I don't know it was an arrangement. Yet, I don't know it was anything but an arrangement. I was positively keen on witnessing what might, how far it would go before one of us shied away."

"Neither of us has recoiled at this point," he replied. "Also, the following stage is a major one."

I was tantalized. We planned to fuck, and it was Mace's thought.

I was diverted and hard throughout the day. I could consider nothing other than covering myself inside Mace. In my life, I had never felt the closeness, the crude weakness, that I felt when I previously entered Lute. What's more, I had not cherished Lute.

That evening, we got right to it. It took work, however I in the end filled him, my pubic hair against his cheeks, my chest against his back, my feet against his feet, my cheek against his cheek, and my hands secured his hands.
I was overpowered. In the event that I had permitted myself, I would have sobbed.

"I love you so much, Carrot," I said.

"I love you as well, Josie."

"What amount?"

"Tons."

I began sliding all through him. I needed to.

I came within him. I was overpowered once more.

"I love you so much," I admitted. I did. Not at all like I had ever cherished another.

I screwed him twice more that evening, including once on his back. Neither of us could look away. I sensed that I could perceive what he was feeling and thinking. I might have remained there, at that time, perpetually, open and defenseless.

That evening, Mace raised unexpectedly the chance of a future together, simply both of us. I realized that would never occur. Regardless of whether I needed it, and I was certain I didn't. I would not be gay.

At the point when Mace made a beeline for New York, I went to Chicago. I utilized Vi and the end of the week to demonstrate to myself that I was not gay. I did to her beginning and end I needed to do and all that she needed me to do. By Sunday morning, I was unable to get hard. I was sexed out. I covered my face between her legs and took her over the edge over and over. On the off chance that I could appreciate doing that, and I did, I was unable to be gay.

All things considered, Mace was never a long way from my brain. Furthermore, I got progressively upbeat as I drove south on 55 toward St. Louis. Each passing mile marker took me closer to Mace and extended my grin.

I was insane with joy when I recovered him from the air terminal. I was unrestrained when he deplaned, embracing and kissing him at the door. I was not an unrestrained individual. Indeed, I was the most focused individual I knew. Mace was testing me.

After sex that evening, I admitted to Mace that I wished the world was where we could remain upbeat and with one another eternity. I didn't reveal to him that I realized it was most certainly not.

The following evening, it was the ideal opportunity for the other shoe to drop. I had denied myself for as long as could be expected under the circumstances, imagining I was a virgin and that I dreaded Mace's size.

I was shocked when Mace rimmed me. It was the move of a veteran, not a novice.

I was additionally excited. I cherished being rimmed.

I gripped as Mace attempted to work me open. I needed to sustain the untruth that I had told.

Mace worked his way in gradually, too gradually. I acted dumb until I was unable to take it any longer.

"Proceed. I need to feel what you feel when I come inside you."

Mace screwed me and afterward sucked me dry. The following morning, he was at me once more, this time while I was on my back. At the point when he hit my prostate, I nearly came all over myself.

We proceeded on like that for the remainder of the mid year. The sex was mind blowing. The affection was better.

Chapter Six

The most recent few days of Mace's mid year brought his companion, Freddie, to visit. I wanted to eat with them on Friday night and afterward drive to Chicago for the end of the week so I could reaffirm my heterosexuality and they could play golf and get up to speed. At the point when I met Freddie, I changed my arrangements, in any event in my brain. He was the most appealing man I had ever found, in actuality. He had unkempt, wavy earthy colored hair, twinkly eyes, and an expansive grin that dissolved volition. I ought to have, however I didn't confide in him and Mace alone for an end of the week.

At the point when I took Mace that evening, I envisioned I was Freddie, conveying myself to him. I took as long as could reasonably be expected, sliding all through him as gradually and as pleasantly as could reasonably be expected.

At the point when Mace took me the following morning, I lost my control. I encouraged Mace on and positively sold out to Freddie that one of us was screwing the other in secret.

I shocked Mace by remaining in St. Louis. I was unable to bear being without him.

As I screwed Mace that evening, I understood I was in a tough situation. I realized we were unable to go on like this eternity, however I likewise realized that I needed to. I was lost in this thing, unrestrained where I never had been.

I was being constrained into trustworthiness dissimilar to ever previously. At the point when Mace expressed gratitude toward me for adoring him, I let it be known was the most straightforward thing I had ever done. At the point when Mace revealed to me he would be lost without me, I beseeched him to "never let me go." I would not joke about this. I knew the vision I had of what my identity was and where I was going was conflicting with an existence with Mace, so I would jolt - or possibly attempt to jolt - sooner or later. I trusted that, when I did, Mace would be sufficiently able to pull me back, to secure me to him, to persuade me regarding what I knew, that existence with him was superior to existence without him, regardless of what an existence with him implied.

I played with the possibility of existence with Mace longer than I anticipated. We went through my third year of graduate school together. We imagined our companions didn't perceive what was evidently noticeable to them, specifically that Mace and I were enamored with one another.

We pondered Mace going through his third year at Georgetown. He was willing, as he completely grasped the possibility of us. I recoiled from the latest possible time, dreading it is equivalent to a public statement. Truly, it couldn't have been whatever else. Regardless of how close the kinship, men didn't get most of the way the nation over for one another in the event that they were not darlings. I would not permit Mace be a Hoya, not make any difference the amount I needed him to be.

We went to Mexico together. While there, Mace disclosed to me he had blown Freddie. I was unable to accuse him. I would have, as well. I was envious, not irate. I was stimulated when he revealed to me its subtleties.

I moved to D.C. It was simpler to mislead myself about Mace when he was not before me consistently. Previously, every time I figured I could stop him, his eyes and his grin persuaded me in any case. I cherished his voice, however it didn't have a similar impact on me when he was miles away.

When he visited for Spring Break, I had talked myself into the end it was the ideal opportunity for me to abandon immature pursuits and to move to the following phase of my life. I needed Mace to be essential for that stage, yet not its star. I was getting back to the limited and straight, by and by. I might want to

235

compose that I chose Mace merited beyond what I might give him, however I had not. I considered myself, not of him.

"You can't have everything," he said. "I'm not going to be your toy."

"I know," I replied. "You have made that understood. . . . At times, I need to get you, take away to an island, and live joyfully ever after."

"We don't need to go to an island to live cheerfully ever after."

"We do."

It was an alternate time. Gay was still significantly out of the standard. Being gay restricted decisions, shut choices, demolished vocations and connections. There were promises of something better, however it was, for unreasonably numerous individuals, a life changing assertion that would never be fixed. Mace was sufficiently able to persevere through that revelation. I was most certainly not. I would not hazard who I intended to be. I would not hazard my relationship with my accomplices. I would not spurn my companions.

"Mace, I am not gay," I dissented. "You might be, yet I am most certainly not. I just can't be."

Mace left the following day. I cried as he did. I understood what I needed to do, and it made meextremely upset to do it.

I considered Mace that evening. Despite the fact that I would not like to, I mentioned to him what I had chosen. I trusted he could and would persuade me I wasn't right. He didn't. He scarcely attempted. He was not as solid as I had urged him to be.

*****

I don't remember a large part of the following two months. I sleepwalked as the days progressed. My weakness sickened me, and I was shattered at the deficiency of Mace.

At the point when Vi visited, she helped me to remember Mace. I related both of them. For quite a while, I had envisioned him when I was within her. I let her go, as well.

Consistently, I got the phone to call Mace. I generally set it back down.

I trusted each time my phone rang that it was he. It never was.

Regardless of how enthusiastically I attempted, I was unable to not consider him. I began seeing him in each blondie man I experienced.

I yielded. I purchased a ticket and headed out to his graduation.

My heart expand when Mace moved in the direction of me. I needed to rush to him, disclose to him I was upset for deserting him, and demand I needed precisely what he needed for us.

I sat tight for him to come to me. I couldn't uncover myself. I was on edge about his response to my unannounced return.

Mace's touch settled my tension. We left the corridor. We kissed. In that kiss, I attempted to share each idea I was thinking, to determine each uncertainty I had.

We rushed back to his loft to have intercourse. I was as destitute as I had ever been. It was superior to it had ever been.

For a little while, my questions were no more. We handily got back to Mark and Mace, Josie and the Carrot. I anticipated our coexistence.

All things considered, I couldn't resist the opportunity to feel that everyone's eyes were on us, recognizing the truth about us. I was unable to stand the investigation. I was unable to be what we were.

At the point when Mace attempted to grasp my hand in a café, I instinctually pulled it back.

At the point when Mace expressed "I love you" on a note or in a letter, I destroyed it.

At the point when Mace inclined his head against my shoulder as we strolled, I really wanted to veer off.

I was a weakling and frail. I needed Mace, however just on my footing, out of the public eye, covered up on display.

I realized Mace would acknowledge those restrictions for some time. Yet, I likewise realized that, eventually, he would compel me to pick. I understood what I would pick. Eventually, I didn't actually have a decision. I was unable to dismiss long periods of reproducing and long stretches of dreaming. I would not pick a prohibited life.

It took Mace not exactly a year to constrain the issue. We were at Freddie's wedding, and Mace became involved with the occasion. He inquired as to whether I would wed him in the event that I could. I needed to state yes. More than anything, I needed to state yes.

It would have been obviously false. I would not wed him. Regardless of whether I could, I would not. I was not prepared for that for which the world was not prepared. I was not happy on the high jump, where all the world could see me. I was unable to get away from what I expected for myself.

He needed to understand what I would reply before he inquired. He must test me. I realized I was falling flat as I said some different option from "yes."

We had intercourse to one another. I realized it was the end. I didn't need it to be, however I realized it was. I needed to hang on. I needed to persuade Mace that getting each other to a great extent would work, that we could make a daily existence through pieces a lot. However, I realized I never could. What I figured would be sufficient for me could never be sufficient for him.

I let him go. To be reasonable for Mace. To allow him to pursue his fantasy. In contrast to the last time, I considered him, not of me.

Chapter Seven

At the point when Mace left, I was certain I was finished with men for good. None could think about, and I didn't need a sorry substitute.

I had met Susan when I moved to D.C. She was clerking a few doors down and was probably the most entertaining individual I had ever met. She was a "wash and go" young lady, glad to pull her hair back and head out, without exertion or cosmetics.

We turned out to be quick companions. She was in a significant distance commitment. Following a couple of months, I revealed to her about Mace. I had never told anybody, and it was an excessive amount to haul around. I needed to tell somebody. Furthermore, I expected to suppress any worry she had that I would not regard her commitment.

At the point when Mace left, she breast fed me through the bitterness. I realized he was on the whole correct to leave, and I was at some level alleviated he had. Yet, I actually throbbed at the deficiency of him.

Susan and I accomplished something pretty much consistently after work. At the point when we not together, we were on the phone. It was not well before we were dating without dating.

In late April, Susan left to visit Andy, the life partner, in New York. I was recovering her Monday morning from National.

I had a hopeless end of the week hanging tight for and without Susan. It actually shocks me how rapidly somebody gets fundamental. You have a full existence without them, you meet them, and afterward you can't recollect how you had a full existence without them. It had been that path with Mace. It was currently that path with Susan.

I halted at an espresso cabin so I would have espresso for her when she moved in. She radiated at me and waved wildly as I pulled up to the check. We halted at a recreation center to have our espresso. We sat opposite one another at an outdoor table. She obviously had a remark, however she would not say it.

"What?" I at last inquired.

"I simply need to state it. I think we need to separate. I know we're not dating. Be that as it may, it seems like it, and it's not reasonable for Andy. I considered all of you end of the week. He realized I was diverted. I enlightened him regarding Mace, to give him some solace. It worked, yet it's as yet not reasonable for me to be with him wanting to be with you."

"What does this separation resemble?"

"We need to quit hanging out."

"That will be intense. Our whole group of friends is the gathering of representatives with whom we work."

"We'll need to split them."

We chatted on, reasonably doing the nonsensical. "What will we do about Friday?" I inquired. Friday was Lisa's birthday, and six of us were going to her home for supper.

"How about we leave it with no guarantees. I figure we can endure one supper."

The week was hopeless—no calls. No visits.

The supper for Lisa began gracelessly. Susan and I stayed away from one another, recognizably. In the event that Susan was in the kitchen, I was in the front room. In the event that I was in the kitchen, Susan was in the lounge.

We found a seat at far edges of the table. We drank an excessive amount of wine. Part of the way through the supper, Susan eliminated her wedding band and set it on the table. I was the first to take note. I caused a stir, and she mouthed "I love you." I stood and left toward her. She stood and strolled toward me. I took her in my arms and, unexpectedly, kissed her. It was a kiss about which individuals talk and compose.

At the point when we separated, the loft was unfilled. Everybody had left. We left, as well. I snatched Susan's ring and took it.

We clasped hands as I headed to her loft. She bobbled with the keys. I didn't know I was to follow her in. She got my hand and pulled me in behind her. I got her and conveyed her to her room. I uncovered her and afterward myself. I realized I would enter her when I could, so I began at her feet. I advanced up her. I took her in my mouth, working her over until she gripped and pulled my hair. I heard her wheeze when I slipped my finger within her. She snared her hands under my arms and pulled me to her mouth. I plunged my tongue in her mouth as she guided me toward her. I kept kissing her as I slid in. She groaned into my mouth. I kept totally as yet, allowing her to change around and to me. I raised up on my arms and began sliding all through her, without rushing. I had not been inside a lady for nearly 12 months.

I had not had the option to make Vi come from infiltration. She said she never had. I needed to utilize my mouth or my hand. Or on the other hand, she needed to utilize her hand while I screwed her.

I made Susan precede I was really close. She curved her neck and pressed her bosoms as she came. I brought down my head and kissed and sucked on her neck. She raised her legs and opened up to me significantly more than she had been. I was as profound as I could go. I snared her knees under my elbows and began driving all through her with reason. My chest hair was smooth with sweat. I trickled between her bosoms. I thickened and afterward dumped, shivering as I came. I delivered her legs, pulled out of her, and moved off of her. Neither of us said a word.

Susan folded into me. She put her mouth to my left side areola and began sucking it. There is an immediate line from my areolas to my dick. I got hard. Susan took me in her grasp, moved over me, and slid down on me. She began shaking to and fro. Each once and once more, she would slide right down, change herself, and afterward grip me with her dividers.

I moved her onto her back, and she attempted with her hands to push me through her. Her entire body shook when she came.

She wheeled around and implored me to take her from behind. I crashed into her.

"Press my tits while you screw me," she demanded. I sat back on my backside, and she followed me. She bolted her hands behind my neck, and I took her tits in my grasp and crushed them,

"Harder," she demanded. I hit into her as hard as Possible.

"Not that," she said. "My tits. Crush them harder."

I did. She shouted out as I kept on driving all through her. We were drenched with sweat when we came. Like her, I cherished it.

*****

At the point when I woke up the following morning, Susan was gone. I discovered her in the kitchen, on the phone. She expressed "Mother" on a bit of paper. She was breaking the "no wedding" news to her mom. I poured espresso and went to the overhang. I thought she required security.

She went along with me about an hour later. "How could that go?" I inquired.

"Better than anticipated," she said. "My folks obviously were never crazy about Andy. They're restless about the conditions, yet they're happy I chosen not to wed him."

"Did you advise him?"

"No, I think I need to do that face to face. I'm flying up one weekend from now."

"I need to go with you."

"No. I need to do this all alone."

We were together the whole week. I went to my condo just to dress for work.

Susan was not normal for any lady with whom I had ever been. She adored sex. She needed to have it constantly. She started it in the event that I didn't.

She contacted me like a person. She put her hands and mouth all over me. As I never had with Vi, I felt wanted.

She preferred giving me head. She was not incredible at it, but rather she was continually willing. She let me ride her face. She let me come in her mouth. She licked my balls. She licked my can. She even fingered it.

At the point when she was truly horny, she beseeched me to screw her butt. She stroked off as I did.

As Friday drew near, I became progressively restless. I contemplated whether Andy could reel Susan back in. I questioned it, yet you never know in issues of the heart. Love back and forth movements.

Susan was made a beeline for the air terminal from work. I would not see her again after Friday morning. I gave her as much as possible Friday morning. I took her over the edge with my tongue and afterward again with my dick. At the point when I was done, I covered her with my sweat-soaked body, remaining within her until I withered and sneaked out.

My uneasiness was superfluous. Susan was back in D.C. mid-evening on Saturday, and Andy was away for acceptable.

We spent the late spring together. In every practical sense, we lived respectively.

At the point when our clerkships finished, I remained in D.C. for a very long time in the Solicitor General's office. Susan made a beeline for a natural non-benefit in Denver. We attempted to see each other each end of the week, regularly meeting in Chicago or St. Louis.

Around a half year after our clerkships finished, Susan called me in the evening. She hosted gone to a commitment get-together that evening. After her companion Ellen had toasted her life partner, he dazed those accumulated by crying and reporting - before everybody - that he was gay and there would be no wedding.

Crying herself, Susan demanded "You need to guarantee you won't ever do that to me."

As she recounted the story, my body loaded up with fear. I made a guarantee I didn't know that I could or would keep.

Chapter Eight

Susan and I were getting hitched in Vail the principal few days of August. I needed Mace to be my best man, however I didn't know how Susan would respond to the thought.

I never discovered. At the point when I skimmed the inflatable past Mace, he popped it, turning me down level. For quite a while, I didn't figure he would even go to the wedding.

Eventually, he did, bringing the person he had been seeing - Juan - with him.

They were at supper Friday night, both in cloth suits, Mace's dim blue and Juan's cream. They made a shocking couple, Mace, fair and brilliant, close to Juan, dull and agonizing.

Susan was anxious to meet Mace. She needed to meet the person who had enticed me to the opposite side of the mountain. He was the just one about whom she knew.

We were at the bar. The four of us stood clumsily together. I was among Mace and Susan, and Mace was among Juan and me. I was intrigued by the incongruity of the situating.

Susan wrestled the second to the ground. She clasped Mace's hand with hers, looked at him straight without flinching, and presented herself.

"Mark has revealed to me about you," she guaranteed him. I had, and I had revealed to Mace I had.

She at that point acquainted herself with Juan, who appeared to be truly awkward. I comprehended. He knew nobody. He was standing up to the affection for Mace's life. He was, I was sure, at a wedding he thought ought not occur.

"Advise me, Mace," I heard Susan murmur. "What did you love most about Mark?"

"It's do, not did," Mace revised her. "What's more, I don't know there's any a certain something. In any case, what I recall most is the way he responded when I revealed to him how my sister had kicked the bucket. It was all generosity, no pity. What's more, he additionally reminded me to live it up. I had not for an exceptionally prolonged stretch of time. Shouldn't something be said about you? What do you love most about him?"

I was keen on her answer. I had never posed her the inquiry.

"I need to stun you and state something risqué like 'how his cum tastes.' But, you'd realize I was lying. It's not delicious. Thus, I'll be straightforward. I most love his eyes. They're wonderful and life-changing. They mention to you his opinion. They sell out him when he lies."

Oh dear, I contemplated internally, as I contemplated whether she was right. I questioned she was. I had disclosed to Mace a ton of untruths, and he had never called any of them out.

Susan and I expected to course. I additionally needed to move her away from Mace. What's more, I expected to move myself away from Mace. At the point when I was close to him, I was not reliable.

Halfway through supper, I saw Mace going to the restroom. Without speculation, I pardoned myself and followed him.

At the point when I entered, Mace was over the sink, washing his hands. I got his attention in the mirror, and he said "Hello you" as he snatched a towel and turned around.

"Hello yourself," I said. I needed to kiss him, so I did. Daintily. At the point when I pulled back, he threw his towel delicately in my face and pushed toward the entryway. I put my hand on it and folded my left arm over his chest.

"Josie, what are you doing?" he inquired.

"I don't have a clue. Yet, I might want to kiss you once more. Without a doubt."

He pivoted, took my face in his, and kissed me hard on the mouth. He attempted to keep his mouth shut, yet I would not permit it. I constrained my tongue into his mouth, and we kissed like we had, quite a long time ago.

252

At the point when we at last separated, I disclosed to him my room number and proposed he go along with me later, when the remainder of the world was sleeping. His solitary reaction was to advise me to remain in the restroom until my dick was not, at this point hard.

He was immersed with Juan as I skimmed back through the room. Susan welcomed my get back with a cocked eyebrow. I grinned at her and put my hand on hers.

She inclined toward me. "Mace looked flushed when he got back from the washroom."

"We had an abnormal experience. He is against this marriage. He thinks I am being unreasonable to you."

"Right?"

"No."

"Is it true that you are sure?"

"Truly. Right?"

"Indeed. I'd be apprehensive if there had been others. Yet, I see how one individual can remove you. I had a companion like that in school. I had never had a lesbian idea, yet I frequently thought about her when I stroked off. I'd have had intercourse with her on the off chance that she had needed."

I was disturbed. I had misled her about "no others." Apparently, she had not seen the lie in my eyes.

"Also," she added. "You're either dependable or you're most certainly not. It doesn't make a difference to me on the off chance that you cheat with a man or a lady. It is important to me in the event that you cheat. You guaranteed you wouldn't. So don't."

Mace didn't thump on my entryway that evening. I accepted and trusted he could simply not move away.

In my inner consciousness, I saw him screwing Juan as I jerked off. Juan was under him, his dull, bristly legs stuck to his chest by Mace's thick, alabaster arms. I came hard as Mace screwed him like a creature, ground-breaking and crude.

Chapter Nine

During the primary year of our marriage, Susan and I put a penny in a container each time we engaged in sexual relations. During the subsequent year, we took a penny out each time we engaged in sexual relations. We deliberately discharged the container a long time before our subsequent commemoration.

Our endeavors prompted Mark Chester Frederick IV. From birth, we called him Chet, which was short for Chester. I recollected that Mace had called his sister Chet. Melissa had become Molester, which had become Chester, Chester the Child Molester, which had become Chet.

Chet subdued Susan's eagerness for sex. Among working and mothering, there was very little an ideal opportunity for intercourse. When there was, it was not, at this point gutsy and lazy. I screwed her rapidly. More often than not, she couldn't have cared less on the off chance that she came. She was giving a source.

I spoke with Mace now and again, typically through email. He furnished scraps of existence with Juan, and I gave pieces of life Susan. They embraced two Colombian young men, Andres and Camilo.

On my 37th birthday celebration, Mace sent me a Happy Birthday email. We expounded to and fro on nothing until Mace asked "Would you say you are dedicated to Susan?"

"I'm," I replied, sincerely. We had been hitched ten years, and I had never broken my guarantee to her.

"Are you?" I asked back.

"I'm not hitched to Susan," he reacted, brazenly. Before I could answer, he added "I'm not dedicated to Juan and he's not devoted to me. We're not prostitutes about it, but at the same time we don't know monogamy is feasible, regardless of whether it's attractive. We attempted it for quite a while. We simply don't lean toward it."

"Do both of you mind?"

"No. I'd mind on the off chance that he went gaga for somebody. He doesn't. I don't all things considered."

"I think your reality and my reality are, as it's been said, completely different."

"Possibly," he reacted, essentially.

I had been enticed. I was as sexual as I had ever been, and Susan's lack of engagement had aroused my curiosity in others.

I had considered every option and long about laying down with Katie, Chet's sitter. She was a DU understudy and a yoga devotee. She was hot and tight and clearly inspired by me. I had numerous odds, as Susan worked extended periods of time and frequently voyaged.

One evening while Susan was away, Katie viewed Chet while I played poker with companions. I showed up home alcoholic and late. Katie was sleeping on the love seat. I left her there and headed to sleep. In the evening, she moved into bed with me. As usual, I was exposed. I was enigmatically mindful of her attempting to get me hard, both with her hand and with her mouth. She fizzled, my intoxication and exhaustion ruining her.

The following morning, I woke up parched and with an awful migraine. I turned up and headed into the washroom. I drank constantly and afterward took four Tylenol and enclosed myself by my robe. I washed my face and glanced in the mirror. I revealed to myself not to do my opinion about doing. I didn't hear myself out.

I got back to the bed. Katie was alert and had the sheet pulled down, uncovering her saucy bosoms. I eliminated the robe and moved into bed. I was on my back close to her. Apprehensively, I arrived at my left hand over and discovered her shaved box. She was dousing wet. Without a word, I moved toward and over her. She took me in her grasp and guided me into her.

"Have you done this previously?" I inquired.

"God, yes," she replied. "I'm 20 years of age."

I slid into her and held consistent. She was tight and warm. She spread her legs wide and covered her face with a pad. I gave her long, slow strokes. She raised her pelvis to meet mine. I sat up on my hindquarters and utilized her knees for influence. I viewed my dick slide all through her and saw her engorged clit. I moved my correct thumb to it and worked her while I watched myself screw her. She shivered when she came, pulling the cushion tight to her face and smothering her clamors.

I came not long after she did, filling her. We had not been cautious.

We didn't talk as we dressed. As she left, she said just "Keep this between you and me."

I needed to fire her as Chet's sitter. Yet, I imagined that may prompt blowback. Thus, I moderate played it, recommending to Susan when she restored that Chet would before long be mature enough to remain without help from anyone else.

Katie sat with Chet a couple of more occasions before we backed her out. The second to last time, I debilitated and screwed her once more. This time, it was the center of the day. Susan was grinding away, Chet was sitting in front of the TV, and I swung by the house to get a few records out of my home office that I had not expected to require. Katie followed me into my office and pulled the entryway shut behind her. While I remained there puzzled, she laid herself level around my work area and pulled her free exercise center shorts aside, uncovering herself me. Without intuition, I unfastened my suit pants, hauled myself out, grabbed hold of her lower legs, and slid into her. I despised myself as I screwed her. Despite how unsuitable my sexual coexistence with Susan had become, I didn't have permit to swindle. In any case, having begun, I was unable to stop.

I got with Katie just a single time after we were done with her. It was an instant message, and it said just "Not pregnant."

I played with enlightening Susan regarding Katie, not to hurt her, but rather to improve a portion of the blame I felt. Eventually, I chose I needed to convey that weight of my selling out alone. I had double-crossed Susan by cheating. I saw no motivation to compound an already painful situation by harming her more.

*****

I had years sooner fallen into a suffering manly relationship with Randy, a person from my rec center. He was an Aryan dream, light haired and blue-looked at. He was taller and preferable worked over I. He was crunchy, with long hair, a whiskered face, and liberal thoughts and goals.

We had met in the rec center. I had seen him when he joined, as had every other person. He was the sort of fellow everybody saw, for valid justifications.

I got some information about his exercise timetable, and I changed mine appropriately. I deliberately ran into him. I nonchalantly referenced that I experienced inspirational issues, and he proposed we work out together so we could consider each other responsible. I felt contemptible.

The most amazing aspect of our morning exercises was our morning showers. Our rec center was old school, with a typical shower with each of the six heads lined along one divider. Randy consistently took the head to the extreme left, and he showered at a 45 degree point to me, zeroed in on the corner.

Randy had a lovely body. His back was built. His midriff was thin. His butt was round and dimpled. His thighs and calves where thick and tangled with hair. Each time he came to behind to cleanser the break of his can, I viewed.

His chest was ripped and covered with straight hair that was more obscure than the hair on his head. His stomach was covered with a similar hair, however not as thickly.

Despite the fact that he attempted, he was unable to shield his groin totally from me. His balls were enormous and hung freely. His dick was normal, in any event delicate.

I never saw him seeing me. I likewise never saw him seeing me seeing him.

We subsided into a mood. On Mondays, Wednesdays, and Fridays, we met at the exercise center and worked out. Randy had a set exercise, and he followed it twistedly. I attempted, however it was hard, and it made me sore.

On Tuesdays, Thursdays, and Saturdays, we met at the recreation center and ran 5 miles together. We barely talked as we ran.

I was unable to sort him out. He was exceptionally appealing, however he never referenced ladies. Or on the other hand men. He didn't gaze at ladies at the rec center. He didn't stare at me in the shower.

Susan inquired as to whether he was gay. I really revealed to her I didn't have the foggiest idea. I conjectured that he might be agamic.

"Perhaps he's an Eunuch," she advertised. I disclosed to her I had seen him exposed. He was unquestionably not an Eunuch.

In spite of the relative multitude of long periods of control and all the time that had passed since Mace, I needed Randy, yet I didn't think he needed me. After the exercise of Thachter, I knew not to press the issue. I needed to hang tight for him to move, on the off chance that he was truly going to.

As we extended one morning, I was squashed that he declared some unacceptable sort of move, to Santa Fe in a quarter of a year. "Work?" I inquired.

"I met somebody. It'squitting any and all funny business. One of us need to move to take it to the following level. I like Santa Fe a ton, so I consented to move."

I was dumbfounded. I felt tears sting my eyes.

"I might want to meet her," I at last offered, when I could.

"She's a he," he replied, unassumingly. I had missed his utilization of "somebody."

"Gracious. I didn't have a clue. You never said."

"I never state. At the point when individuals begin revealing to me they're straight, I'll begin disclosing to them I'm gay."

"I'm straight."

"I'm gay."

We began our run. As we did, I chose to inform Randy regarding Mace, not to make him agreeable, but rather to perceive what he would do or say.

At the point when we were once again at our vehicles and chilling off, I plunged. "I had a beau once. At the point when I was in graduate school."

"I'm astonished. You appear to be too grave to even consider having gone for a stroll on the wild side, what with your Roman numerals and dignified estate and wonderful spouse and significantly more amazing child."

"It astounded me, as well," I replied, to some degree honestly. "What's more, overpowered me. I cherished him a great deal. As a matter of fact, I adored him really. He needed us to last. I was unable to let it."

"That is really awful. Genuine affection is elusive."

"It is."

"Yet, you discovered it again with Susan."

"I did," I said. I don't know that he trusted me. I don't know that I trusted myself.

As usual, we shook hands as we separated. "I will miss you," I guaranteed him.

"I'll miss you, as well."

I told Susan when I was back home. Randy was woven into our family. He was my closest companion. He was likewise Chet's closest companion. He had spent endless hours in our home. He was the lone individual Chet had requested to rest over.

"Two things," I declared as I took off my sweat-soaked garments. "One, Randy is moving. To Santa Fe. Two, he is moving to be with a person. The secret is tackled. He is gay."

"How long have you known?"

"About which one?"

"Both. By the same token."

I checked the time. "55 minutes. To both. He disclosed to me he was moving today before our run. I asked 'why.' He said he met somebody. I asked her name, and he said 'she's a he.' I was paralyzed."

"What's his name?"

"I don't have a clue. I didn't inquire."

"Truly?"

"Truly."

"Your closest companion discloses to you he's leaving town for a man and you don't think to ask the man's name?"

"I surmise not."

I thought I heard "narcissist" as she left. It would not have been the first occasion when she alluded to me as one. It was anything but a commendation. The pressure between us was genuine. We had floated from one another, bound together now by Chet and by the guarantees we had made when we wedded one another.

Our marriage was just a sad remnant of what it used to be. Like I stated, we were once in a while sexual. At the point when we were, it was constantly started by me, and it was repetition.

Our lack of engagement in sex persisted to our day by day lives. We lived respectively, yet we were having separate existences. We shared an interest in our child, yet in essentially nothing else. What she didn't provide for Chet, she provided for her companion Gillian (with a hard "G," which deliberately would not articulate). What I didn't provide for Chet, I need to Randy.

*****

Six of us from the exercise center went out to say goodbye to Randy. He was not leaving for 2.5 months, so this was the start of what we warmly called's "long farewell."

The night finished early. Everything except Randy had a family or a spouse to whom they expected to return home.

I drove Randy to his structure. He welcomed me in for a "last." Randy had a breathtaking perspective on midtown from his gallery, and we tasted scotch and smoked stogies while we appreciated it.

All of a sudden, Randy inquired as to whether I had delighted in gay sex when I was doing it.

"A few sections," I reacted, honestly.

"Like what?"

"Well . . . . I preferred getting blown. Mace gave preferable head over any young lady I have ever had. Furthermore, I enjoyed screwing him. He was so smooth thus close."

"Spoken like a genuine straight."

"In what way?"

"Obviously you enjoyed getting blown and screwing."

"Do you not?"

"Obviously. Each person does. In any case, I would prefer to blow somebody than get blown. Furthermore, I'd preferably get screwed over fuck."

"Indeed, we would be wonderful together, at that point."

"Would it be advisable for us to discover?"

The move at last made, my mouth went dry. Not hanging tight for an answer, Randy stood and held out his hand to me. I felt like a recuperating alcoholic, enticed after such countless years to take that first beverage once more. I had since quite a while ago needed Randy, and he was not too far off before me, offering himself to me, an open jug of whiskey.

I attempted to oppose, yet I proved unable. I put my hand in his and let him lead me to his room.

He ventured into the restroom and flipped the switch, which lit his room barely enough cap I could see. At the point when he returned, I was unable to move. I was hypnotized. I watched him strip. As he gazed at me, he gradually unfastened his shirt and opened it, uncovering that tangled chest I for such a long time had yearned to contact.

Without taking off his shirt totally, he unfastened his pants, opened them, and let them tumble to the floor. He ventured out of them and afterward utilized his feet to pull each sock off.

"Goodness my God," I stated, as he remained before me in white fighter briefs and an open plaid shirt. "You resemble a model. You don't look genuine."

"I'm genuine," he stated, strolling toward me as he pulled his arms from his shirt and dropped it to the floor.

I began to unfasten my shirt, yet Randy dominated. He continued gazing at me as he unfastened and opened my shirt. As he licked and sucked my chest, he opened my pants and brought down them past my hips. He advanced down me, bringing down my pants as he put his hot mouth on my hard dick through my fighters. I brought down my fighters and ventured out of my pants. At the point when I did, Randy folded his mouth over me. I peered down and watched him suck me. I moved my hands to his light hair and coordinated his cadence. I watched myself screw his face.

"Goodness, Jesus," I said. "I will come."

As opposed to pull off, Randy added his hand and took me over the edge in his mouth. I twisted around and prepared myself against his shoulders as he depleted all I needed to give.

It had been excessively long. I dove on Randy's dick, sucking him as he sat on the floor. He added his hand and I moved my mouth with it. I was too eager to even think about reading the signs, and I was alarmed when I heard him snort and begin to come in my mouth. I choked a little as I attempted to swallow and continue onward. I pulled off, and Randy completed against my chest.
We moved to the bed. Randy ate my butt while he sat tight for me to bob back. I squirmed under his unpleasant, wet tongue.

Randy sheathed and lubed me and afterward demanded I take him on his back. I slid effectively into him and began voraciously screwing him. He snared his hands under his knees and tested his sanity toward his chest. At the point when he did, I entered him as profoundly as Possible. I was in to the base when I came, shivering and sweat-soaked. Randy came, as well, covering his chest and stomach with thick, splendid white liquid.

"I generally thought about what that would resemble," he stated, after I sneaked out of him and eliminated the condom.

"How was it?" I inquired.

"Worth the pause."

"I wish we had not paused," I conceded.

"Me, as well. In the event that you had said something sooner, I probably won't be moving to New Mexico."

"You would. I'm hitched."

"Right."

I declared I expected to get moving, pulled on my fighters, and went to the washroom. At the point when I restored, my pants and shirt were collapsed on the bed, and my socks were from my perspective. I dressed and set out toward the entryway.

"Hello," Randy called out from the kitchen. "Hang on a second."

I turned and held up at the entryway. "We're doing this sort of in reverse," he said. "However, in the event that we don't kiss, at that point this is simply going to some sort of wham bam fuckfest, and I need it to be more than that."

He kissed me. I kissed him back, maneuvering him into me as hard as could be expected under the circumstances.

Our eyes were open, as we kissed. I left without saying a word.

We quit running and working out. Rather than meeting Randy at the exercise center or the recreation center, I went to his structure and to his room. He sucked my dick and I sucked his. I screwed him, however he never screwed me. He never at any point proposed the subject.

We quit utilizing condoms. Randy needed to feel me spill in him, and I idiotically thought I was protected in the event that I was the one doing the screwing.

After a month, we were frantically infatuated with one another. It resembled it had been with Mace. I was most joyful when my head was on his chest. I enjoyed tuning in to his heart beat. I preferred his hand in my hair.

I found each motivation to end up with him. We disappeared for a fly fishing end of the week. Our lines never got wet. We were working out and running perseveringly, yet we both put on weight.

A month from that point forward, Randy offered to remain in Denver. "Simply give the signal," he said.

I ought to have. I didn't. Similarly as with Mace, I just proved unable.

Upset by my dread, Randy moved the next Saturday to be with Matt, the "somebody" he had referenced toward the beginning of our excursion. My family was with me to bid farewell. Susan went first. Randy demanded that she cause me to be acceptable. I thought she had no clue he had caused me to be awful.

Chet went second. The two of them cried as they embraced. Randy and Chet had since quite a while ago shared an exceptional bond. Chet alluded to Randy as his "closest companion, other than my father."

I went last. Randy murmured "I love you" in my ear. I ought to have said "I love you, as well," however I didn't. I said "sure" all things being equal. I could see that Randy was injured when I pulled away.

As I drove my family home, I thought we had pulled off everything. We had been attentive, and Susan appeared to be unaware.

I thought wrong. Susan suprised me that evening in bed. "You broke your guarantee, didn't you?"

"No," I lied.

"Try not to lie, Mark. I could see it all over today. I watched sweethearts part. Disclose to me I'm off-base."

I stopped. I looked at Susan without flinching. I felt tears sting my eyes. I chose to quit lying. "You are not off-base."

"How long would you say you were two sweethearts?"

"We were not sweethearts," I lied once more.

"You're a liar. I understand what I saw today."

I multiplied down. "We were not darlings. We dawdled a tad. Simply the most recent month or two."

"Month or two?" She asked, drawing out the two, so it was the longest word I had ever heard. "Did you screw him? Did he screw you?"

"Susan, don't do this. You don't need or need the subtleties."

"That implies yes. Kindly disclose to me you were protected."

I didn't react.

"Mark?"

I actually didn't react. I proved unable.

"Goodness my God, Mark. You screwed me toward the beginning of today. With no condom. You could be debilitated from him and making me wiped out. Is it true that you are actually that freaking egotistical?"

Evidently, I was. I had not considered her one time I had intercourse to Randy, exposed.

"Have there been others?" she inquired. I didn't reply, which was an answer.

"Men or ladies or both?" she inquired.

"Only one . . . . A lady."

"Who?"

"Susan, it doesn't make a difference what it's identity was. It simply matters that it was."

"Who right? I reserve an option to know."

"Fine. It was Katie. It just happened twice."

"Katie?! As in Chet's sitter? She's a screwing youngster, Mark. You are extraordinary."

"It was simply sex."

"Just a man would state that," she rebuked me. "As though it should cause me to feel better that you just screwed her, rather than having intercourse to her. . . . Furthermore, it was not 'simply sex' with Randy, and you know it. You were enamored with him some time before you began screwing him. I attempted to imagine I didn't perceive what I saw, however I saw it. . . . You truly are a screwing narcissist."

My life washed away. At last outfitted with motivation to do as such, Susan requested that I leave. I did. She demanded full guardianship of Chet and half of all the other things in return for her quietness. I surrendered. I required her quiet. I was unable to have the world know why we were separating.

I saw Randy once after the separation. He headed out to Denver to visit companions. I welcomed him to remain with me. He faltered prior to yielding. The primary evening, we stayed in bed separate beds. I laid conscious excessively long contemplating whether he would go along with me. He didn't.

The subsequent evening, I welcomed him to share my bed. He reacted that he didn't figure it is reasonable for Matt. I was frustrated, however concealed it in faked detachment. We drank and talked. I wished so anyone can hear that he had been more open when he lived in Denver. He conceded that he wished the equivalent.

At the point when the time had come, he settled his reservations and followed me to my room. I uncovered totally and moved into bed. He attempted to leave his clothing on, yet I would not permit it. "Those, as well," I scolded.

When we were under the covers, we deserted all misrepresentation of hesitance.

I sucked him as hard as could reasonably be expected. I gulped all that moved from him.

When he bobbed back, he screwed me unexpectedly. I was on my stomach, and he floated over me, beating all through me. I felt him swell and afterward fill me. I was splashed with sweat.

We went at one another again the following morning before his trip out. We kissed. We sucked each other in a 69. I took Randy on his back. I shouted out when I came.

He took me remaining against the divider. I came when he did, splattering the consumed orange paint with ropes of cum.

At the point when he left, I was amped up for our future. I was sure I could have with him what I had needed with Mace, a straight life to the public eye with a man as an afterthought.

I never saw Randy again. I worried when he didn't answer my calls or my writings, dreading Matt had found what we had done. I ought to have been apprehensive, yet not of that. Following a couple of days, a peculiar voice addressed Randy's telephone. It was his sister. She unassumingly educated me that

Randy was dead, having been killed by a smashed driver in a late morning auto collision. He was Matt's traveler and took the brunt of the effect. Matt was injured, however not mortally.

I took Chet to his companion's memorial service. I gave the funeral director an envelope to sneak through Randy's urn. The note inside contained the four words I ought to have revealed to him when he left Denver for Sante Fe. Or then again that I ought to have used to prevent him from leaving by any means.

"I love you, as well."

Chapter Ten

My subsequent marriage was brief. I met Alexis at a pledge drive for a senate up-and-comer in 2006. She was dull and steamy and puzzling. Her significant other had been rich stunning and a Republican bundler. At the point when he kicked the bucket, she acquired his abundance and his political commitments.

I was the last individual went out. I was the financier for the applicant's mission, so I remained behind to gather the checks and the promises. Alexis came down the stairs in a silk robe and proposed we end the night with a scotch on the veranda. We finished it in her bed all things being equal. She rode me heartlessly, with an enthusiasm and a life that misrepresented her 51 years.

I became involved with the tornado of cash and sex. Both appeared to be interminably accessible. We traveled to intriguing puts on her private plane. We engaged in sexual relations as we flew.

I requested that she wed me after just two months. She said truly, and we flew the following end of the week to Bora and wedded each other on a sea shore.

I rapidly lamented my carelessness. Alexis was accustomed to getting her direction. She bossed me like a kid. She would not like to find out about, considerably less see, my kid.

She attempted to drive me to stop working, so I would be accessible to her at whatever point she needed. At the point when I won't, she reached one of the named accomplices of my firm and encouraged him to vacation me.

I demanded she chill out. At the point when she cannot, I moved out. She responded by separating from me.

Our marriage was finished, just a short time after it began, and just a brief time after I had met her unexpectedly. The consummation was kind to us both.

*****

After two years, Mace messaged he would be in Denver for work. We met at the Brown Palace, where he was remaining.

He very quickly got some information about the nonattendance of my wedding band. I said just "That is finished." I didn't reveal to him how long it had been finished, or that I had been hitched again since.
"What occurred?"

"It doesn't make a difference," I stated, contemptuously and with a tone that proposed he ought not raise the issue once more.

He was getting back to Denver fourteen days after the fact for three days of gatherings. We made arrangements to meet for supper on his last night around. We snickered and thought back as we arranged.

Mace was maturing admirably. "You look like Keith Urban in your mature age," I said.

"Much obliged to you. That is high applause. He's beautiful."

"You are, as well."

"You resemble the person from Office Space, just with blue eyes."

"Ron Livingston. I have gotten that previously. He isn't ravishing."

"He is to me. You are, as well. Still."

I covered his hand with mine. I saw that he didn't pull it away.

At the point when supper was finished, I offered to drive him back to his inn. In transit, I inquired as to whether he needed to see my new home, a cottage on Washington Park. On the off chance that he said truly, I would constrain him to remain the evening.

He said yes. We drank and talked. At the point when it was the ideal opportunity for Mace to leave, I would not drive him. I revealed to him I was too smashed to even consider driving and that he could flag down a taxi or stay the evening. I was plotting, and I think he knew it.

Mace demanded the subsequent room. I thrashed around momentarily and afterward chose to stop messing around. Bare, I strolled to his room, thumped, and welcomed myself in.

I was immediate. I sat confronting him on the bed, my hard on self-evident. "Let us not imagine this will occur," I stated, bringing my mouth down to his.

"I have missed you," I murmured in his mouth. "I was sitting across that table from you and watching your eyes dance and everything I could consider was kissing your lips."

We went back as expected. We kissed a lot and kissed until he raised up and pulled his fighters off.

"I need to have intercourse to you," I murmured. Mace didn't react verbally. He pulled me down on top of him and raised his legs. I ventured into the end table, pulled out a condom and lube, and was rapidly within him. Mace gazed at me as I conveyed myself to him, again and again. Fifteen years washed away.

"You feel so great," I said.

"You do as well."

"I have missed this."

"Me, as well."

I continued onward. I had been having a huge measure of sex in my single life, and my control had gotten incredible. I could be persevering, in the event that I needed to be.

I would not like to be. I needed to come inside Mace, similar to I had so often such countless years back. I angled my back and began pummeling into him. I snorted and came, over and over, filling the condom. I fell, covering Mace with my sweat-soaked body.

"That was an immense climax," I said.

"I know. I could tell."

"Did you come?"

"No."

"I need you to come in my mouth," I stated, following a way to his dick with my tongue and deceiving my aversion of cum. I worked him with my hand and my mouth.

284

He came hard, again and again. I gulped as I kept at him, depleting and gulping everything except the last drop. I gave that back to him, off my tongue after I had gotten back to his mouth and begun kissing him once more. We nodded off.

The following morning, I inquired as to whether I could ride him. He replied "obviously."

I returned down on him to prepare him. I was covering him with my spit.

"Don't we need a condom?" he inquired.

"No. I confide in you."

"We need a condom," he replied. He plainly didn't confide in me.

I ventured into the end table and pulled out a magnum. I moved it on him, ridden him, and afterward slid gradually down as far as Possible. Riding Mace resembled riding a bike.

I rode Mace as hard as could be expected under the circumstances. He moved me away from and onto me without pulling out. He remained close to the bed, held my legs level against my chest, and screwed me as hard and as quick as I had ever been screwed.

"Try not to come inside me," I said. "I need you to come in my mouth once more." Mace realized I didn't care for cum. I was attempting to communicate the amount I needed him by taking what I didn't care for from him.

Mace pulled out and pulled the condom off. I mixed to the top of the bed. Mace rode me and screwed my face. He came so hard thus much that I choked, cum running down my jawline.

Mace licked my jaw, kissed me, and took me in his grasp. As he sucked my tongue, I came.

Mace moved his trip back and we went through the day in bed. It was much the same as bygone eras.

I drove Mace to the air terminal. I contemplated whether he would return.

Before he left the vehicle, I asked "Do you actually consider how our lives would have ended up on the off chance that we had quite recently continued onward?"

"No," he stated, unassumingly. "I'm carrying on with that life, only not with you."

"Well played, Carrot," I stated, as my heart broke and dissipated. "Well played."

Chapter Eleven

I attempted marriage once again, only to look good. I went the other way of Alexis. Michelle was 15 years more youthful than I and came from an exceptionally small foundation. From numerous points of view, she helped me to remember Mace. She was savvy and independent, unassuming and hesitant.

She was extremely conventional. She was not a virgin, but rather she pushed sex with me off until we were hitched. We had intercourse unexpectedly on our wedding night. She was bad at it, and she didn't care for it.

I couldn't have cared less. This marriage was for comfort and window dressing. I required a mother to Chet, who had come to live with me full-time when his mom quit Denver and moved to her family's home in Southhampton. It was 2011. He was 15.

Michelle required a steady base. She was keen however terrified. She dreaded she was unable to make it all alone. I was 44 and effective. I was a wellbeing net.

Michelle and Chet improved than she and I. They venerated one another. I was the oddball in my own home.

One year into our marriage, Michelle and I were in various rooms on various floors. At the point when I was intrigued, she yielded to me, inside specific limits. I was unable to go down on her, and she would not go down on me. I could finger her clitoris, however I was unable to slide a finger within her. I could screw her, yet just in the event that I had gotten myself close so the genuine entrance was brief. I needed to wear a condom.

I seldom was keen on sex with her. It was awful. Also, I had been having a covert illicit relationship with Lin, a youthful partner in our office, for as long as year. Lin's family had emigrated from China before his introduction to the world. He had gone to Stanford for both school and graduate school, had clerked on the Ninth Circuit, and was currently a subsequent year partner in our firm. He was in all likelihood gay, however he was profoundly in the storage room. Gay was not a satisfactory life in China or in the brains of his folks. He had never frustrated them. He was not going to begin now.

Other than Lute, I was not normally pulled in to dull hair and dim eyes. I favored reasonableness, similar to Mace and Randy.

Be that as it may, I considered Lin the whole day I met him. There was an euphoria in his face that couple of had.

After two days, I wound up visiting his office. I had composed a task just to have something to discuss.

Lin was evil brilliant, and I got him engaged with each bit of suit I was driving. I didn't have to. I needed to. I needed to have motivation to see him.

We went to New Orleans together to remove a specialist in a patent encroachment case. Lin's preliminary work was exceptional. I destroyed the master on questioning. The Court could never affirm him. Lin and I commended our great day at Mother's and afterward on Bourbon Street.

Lin recommended a last beverage in the bar. I concurred. One beverage went to two and we wound up having three last beverages.

In the lift to our floor, Lin rearranged gracelessly and afterward inclined toward the divider. He looked at me straight without flinching and grinned. I perceived the look as one of the seven dangerous sins - desire.

Our rooms were three entryways separated. We took a gander at one another, bungled with our keys, opened our entryways, and went into our rooms. While Lin was taking a gander at me, I had needed to ask him in for a fourth last beverage. At last, I concluded I proved unable. My standing was unblemished, at any rate grinding away.

I had stripped and move into bed when I thought I heard a light thump on my entryway. I got up, pulled on my fighters, and went to the entryway. I could see Lin through the peephole. He was wearing the inn's robe.

I opened the entryway a break. "What do you need, Lin?"

"I needn't bother with anything. I just idea perhaps you needed some organization. Or then again another beverage."

"I don't need another beverage," I replied. I purposefully didn't make reference to organization.

Lin ventured into my room. "Me, it is possible that," he murmured.

"At that point what do you need?" I inquired.

"This," he stated, getting me through my fighters.

I stuck Lin to the mirror. "This needs to remain between you and me," I murmured as I unfastened the robe.

"You have my statement."

I kissed him. He was little, perhaps 5'6" and 140 pounds. He was constructed like an athlete.

I got him and attempted to drop him on the bed. He stuck around my neck like an insect monkey and pulled me down on top of him. As we kept on kissing, he utilized his feet to pull my fighters down. He immediately had his hands on me. He crawled down me, sucking my areolas and kissing my stomach prior to taking me in his mouth. He was gifted. He brought me down his throat to the base and drained me with his tongue and his throat muscles. I moved left so he could take control. He did. He sucked me with desert. I came hard, filling his mouth. He kept at me, sucking and gulping until I was too touchy to even consider taking any more.

I pulled him to my face and kissed him. "Take your clothing off."

He did. His dick was normal, which was more than I had anticipated. Bits of gossip about Asian men went before him to my bed.

I stuck him to the bed. His body was rigid, yet his skin was strikingly delicate. I kissed my way to his crotch and was going to take him in my mouth when he reported "I don't care for that . . . Screw me all things considered."

I got a condom from my things, moved it on, and moved back up his body. I sucked his neck as he stressed for my dick. I slipped into him. He adored getting screwed. His body arced and stressed. He asked me on, imploring me for more and to accelerate.

I lost all sense of direction in his words. I came as he implored me to screw him quicker, harder, longer. He came when I had, without contacting himself. He spread his cum everywhere on his chest and stomach, pulled the sofa up over us, and turned his back to me. I slid in behind him.

The following morning, I asked how he could be gay dislike sensual caresses. "I don't have the foggiest idea," he reacted. "I simply don't. By any means. I'd preferably get screwed quickly. Furthermore, I come without fail."

We didn't talk at work. I visited his loft routinely. I loved standing while he blew me. I enjoyed watching his dim, full lips slide here and there the shaft of my dick. He loved watching me watch him.

He could spread his legs level on a bed, opposite to his body. At the point when he did, he was totally open. He cherished being screwed, and I adored screwing him. He had muscles in his rear end that I never knew existed. He utilized them to encourage me on and to stop me.

He never screwed me. The possibly time I sucked him was the point at which he would drape his head over the edge of the bed, and I would slide totally down his throat. His dick would be in my face as I screwed his face, and each once in for a little while the inclination to blow him conquered me. I would suck him until I came. He never came from me sucking him.

Like with Lute, we were not sweethearts. We were creatures, meeting for fleshly demonstrations of desire and afterward isolating. The solitary night we spent together was that first evening.

*****

Chet satisfied me by choosing to follow me to Yale. The week prior to his secondary school graduation, he came out to me. I had been dubious. He was 6'4", very much assembled, and attractive, yet he had never at any point referenced a young lady.

At the point when he came out to me, I encouraged him not to settle on the decision he was making: he demanded it was anything but a decision. I demanded it was. I considered myself I did. In my psyche, I had decided not to be gay.

I sent him to a specialist, trusting she could persuade him he was not what he thought he was. She was an exercise in futility and cash. She concurred it was anything but a decision and asked him to go up against me every single time I proposed something else.

I could feel Chet floating away from me. I accused his advisor, not my atavism.

I chose to go see her. She guaranteed me she was unable to converse with me about what she discussed with Chet. I guaranteed her I would not like to discuss that, yet rather needed to have a philosophical conversation with her.

I began seeing her week after week. I informed her concerning Adam and Lute and Mace and Susan and Randy and Alexis and

Michelle and Lin. I disclosed to her the sane decisions I trusted I had made along the way of my life. I praised the strength I had appeared by dismissing an existence with Mace and an existence with Randy. I guaranteed her Chet could settle on similar decisions on the off chance that he developed a similar strength I had.

She demanded what I praised as strength was really shortcoming. "It would have taken strength," she stated, "to buck assumptions and standards and pick Mace, whom you have depicted as the affection for your life. You were excessively feeble. You denied yourself of the affection for your life out of shortcoming, not out of solidarity."

"I'm not gay," I demanded.

"Possibly not," she said. "In any case, you are likewise not straight. You can deceive yourself, however your life isn't the life of a straight man. At least, you are promiscuous. I'd portray you as gay. You have had three extraordinary loves. Two were men. One was a lady. You lost the affection for that lady over the adoration you had for a man. You're a shrewd man, Mark. What does that advise you?"

I kept on countering her. I would not acknowledge her investigation or her analysis. In any case, I continued returning.

295

The more I saw her, the more I expected that Chet had by one way or another, someway gotten something from me thus thought being gay was an adequate decision for him to make. It was 2014, and the world was tremendously unique in relation to it had been 20 years before while picking Mace would have been so important.

I would not concur that individuals were brought into the world gay. I thought homosexuality was conduct, not inborn.

She oppose this idea. She demanded an abstinent gay was as yet a gay. She likewise demanded that my obliviousness was the boundary among me and my child.

"It is anything but a decision he's making. However long you imagine something else, Chet will keep on floating from you."

I was vexed. On the off chance that I demanded she wasn't right, I gambled losing Chet. On the off chance that I acknowledged she was correct, I gambled standing up to a day to day existence of mixed up self-hardship and shortcoming.

I was unable to lose Chet. I would never neglect my child.

I chose to drive Chet to Yale. We went through 20 hours together in the vehicle. I revealed to him I was upset for attempting to compel him to be something he was most certainly not. I disclosed to him I adored him, regardless. I informed him concerning Mace and the decision I had made. I disclosed to him I had adored his mom profoundly. I revealed to him I had lost her since I had fallen head over heels in love for his companion Randy. I revealed to him I had never adored Alexis or Michelle. I informed him concerning Lin, and that I had never cherished him, all things considered.

Chet revealed to me he cherished me. He revealed to me he didn't care for being "Chet"; he needed to be Mark, similar to me, and planned to pass by Mark at Yale. He inspired everything about could recollect about Mace. He was furious about Randy; his fondness for Randy had been his first notion that he was gay. He revealed to me he had never preferred Alexis and felt sorry for Michelle. He is demanded I needed to leave her. Furthermore, Lin. He urged me to attempt to recover Mace before it was past the point of no return.

We went through the end of the week in New York City. We visited exhibition halls and displays. We went for long strolls. We talked like old companions.

I cried constantly when I dropped him at Yale and as I drove back to Denver. I planned to miss him. Yet, more than that, I begrudged him. He was solid where I had been feeble. He was nearly the existence I ought to have had.

Chapter Twelve

Michelle and I discreetly separated from that Fall. We sold the house. I purchased every one of us a condo in Cherry Creek. I consented to make regularly scheduled installments for a very long time, a similar measure of time we had been hitched.

I was overwhelming fifty. I was threefold separated and alone.

I had quit laying down with Lin. It was base and insufficient.

It had been a long time since I had seen Mace, yet he was everything I could consider. I saw him in each blondie head, in each wry grin.

I needed to take my child's recommendation and check whether I could acknowledge what I had dismissed, yet I had no clue about how. Or then again on the off chance that I ought to. Some portion of me felt that boat had cruised, Mace had Juan, and I should let them be, make an effort not to upset what I might have had.

Another piece of me recalled that dull room in the rear of a rent loft in University City, to when it was only both of us, to when there was such a lot of adoration it cleared away alert and show and assumption and dread. It was only the Carrot and Josie, two young men in adoration.

"You're not kidding," my child advised me during our week by week call.

"I don't think so. I'm making an effort not to sort out the correct activity."

"I don't think so. You're worrying. You're apprehensive he may state no. You're much more apprehensive he may state yes."

"Consider the possibility that he says no."

"At that point you'll feel the torment he felt when you didn't pick him. It'll hurt. Yet, you'll get it over. Furthermore, you'll proceed onward. What's more, you won't need to spend the remainder of your life thinking about what he would have said in the event that you had offered yourself to him."

"Consider the possibility that he says yes."

"At that point you will see whether you can develop old with him, at long last upbeat, at long last genuine."

"When did you get so brilliant?"

"I've generally been keen. I'm at Yale. All alone. Not as a heritage."

He was correct. He had would not allow me to help him. He had acquired his way in as an understudy, not as an inheritance. Furthermore, he was flourishing.

He was not an individual from the Tory Club. He was more Socialist than Tory. He was studying Economics, since he needed saw how the first class ran the world. Not to go along with them. To bring them down.

He was infatuated with Charles, a Sudanese man he met as I drove away from New Haven. They were on a similar floor in the Silliman, my old school. They found each other in the corridor. It was unexplainable adoration. They immediately exchanged flat mates and had been living respectively the whole year.

I met Charles over Christmas. Chet - I would easily forget to call him Mark - brought him out to ski. We leased a house in Vail and went through seven days there.

Charles was taller and less fatty than Chet. His skin was a profound, rich earthy colored. His eyes were dark. He kept his hair incredibly close. His face was precise. He was pretty, in the manner in which a few men are. The magnificence of his skin and the points of his face helped me to remember Grace Jones.

He was slender and ripped from football (theirs, not our own) and running. He talked the Queen's English in a profound, thunderous voice.

His family had moved from the Sudan when he was thirteen and they sorted out he was gay. They dreaded mistreatment. Furthermore, AIDS.
Charles and Chet helped me to remember Mace and me. At the point when they took a gander at one another, affection spilled out. Charles took a gander at Chet like he was a wonder, a disclosure. Chet saw Charles like he was his number one thing ever.

I needed to be youthful once more, to know then what I knew now. I needed to be 25 out of 2015, not in 1990. I needed Mace back.

I chose a fantastic signal. I explored San Blas, where we had spent those thoughtless weeks in 1991 and 1992, when consistently was loaded up with probability. Our beachfront lodging was as yet open. From what I could see on the web, San Blas had not changed much in the a long time since our last visit. The new century had not ventured that far into Mexico.

I would turn fifty on February 17. I purchased a departure from Denver to Mazatlan for February 16. I purchased a departure from San Diego to Mazatlan for the exact day. I would land three hours before Mace, on the off chance that he came.

I asked Mace through email for his location. It was nearly Christmas. He would think it was to send a card.

I printed the agenda, collapsed it conveniently, and put it in an envelope. I added a basic note.

Carrot:

It has been excessively long.

I'm not an idiot any longer.

I need to spend (in any event) my 50th birthday celebration with you.

Come immediately.

Josie

I realized he would get the "Come without a moment's delay" reference. It was from Wodehouse, which we used to peruse to one another. Quite a long time ago.

I realized Mace realized I didn't need him to advise me ahead of time on the off chance that he was coming or not. It was not the manner in which we were.

I was a mix of nerves as I voyaged south on February 16. In the course of recent weeks, I had switched back and forth between persuading myself Mace would show and persuading myself he would not. My equivocations changed by day and disposition.

Chet was overjoyed. He loved that I was dubious and powerless. He likewise enjoyed the great motion. He was sure Mace would show. He was sure the story couldn't end some other way.

I was at the entryway for Mace's flight, moving anxiously from foot to foot. I watched the plane taxi in and stop. It seemed like a very long time before a traveler arose. I had purchased a top notch ticket, so - in the event that he was on the flight - he would be one of the principal travelers off.

My expectation ebbed as many travelers deplaned. There were too much. Families came out. Top notch must be vacant. I was squashed. I had become tied up with the fantasy.

Similarly as I was going to turn and leave, Mace was at the entryway, actually looking a lot of like Keith Urban. At the point when he saw me, he radiated. At the point when I saw him, I took off. I rushed to him, folded my arms over him, and kissed him with all that I had. I didn't mind who saw.

"Gracious my God, Mace. Such countless individuals had gotten off. I thought you were not coming."

"I exchanged my seat. I permitted that older Mexican lady to take my top of the line seat and I sat down, in the rear of mentor."

"Obviously you did," I said. Obviously he had. He was generally so Mace.

I was grinning so hard I figured my face would break. I was so brimming with expectation and love I figured I may detonate.

I maneuvered Mace into me. I needed to fashion us into one. He was definitely more strong than I recollected.

My telephone hummed. It was Chet, messaging.

"Well?"

"That's right."

":)"

As we drove south to Tepic and afterward west to San Blas, I realized there had been no show in San Diego upon the receipt of my greeting. Mace had not picked me over Juan. Truth be told, Juan had moved with their young men to Bogota right around a year sooner. Juan was doctoring in his folks' previous facility, persuaded he expected to give something back to his country. The young men were joined up with the National University, having chosen they needed to re-visitation of their country to complete their schooling.

Juan and Mace were as yet hitched, however they didn't see each other much. In their year separated, Mace had made three outings to Bogota. Juan had not gotten back to the states.

Mace had gone into their marriage needing the conventional idyll of loyalty and monogamy. Juan had not, accepting they were unnatural states constrained upon individuals to sabotage want and any unintended outcomes of that want. Juan had surrendered to Mace's goals for the initial segment of their marriage, and Mace had yielded to Juan's for the later part. Mace preferred Juan's goals better; they were simpler to accomplish.

As we drove, the a long time since I had last seen him and the a long time since I had injured him vanished. Like a most loved old sweater at the lower part of a cedar chest, "Mace and Mark" had just been lost. Rediscovered, we fit each other easily and heartily.

It was late when we looked into our lodging and sunk into our room. It had been a taxing day of movement.

Mace needed to wash the three day weekend. He got back from the shower enclosed simply by a towel. He had been occupied. His muscles undulated. His muscle to fat ratio was non-existent.

I had not been so focused. As I quite often had, I was conveying at any rate ten pounds I didn't need.

Mace dropped the towel and slid into bed. We kissed. It was sorcery, much the same as it generally had been.

I pulled away and revealed to Mace I planned to shower. At the point when I was done, he was snoozing on his left side, twisted into a ball. I pulled the sheet over us and slid in behind him. We laid down with the light on.

I arose first on my birthday. I was formally fifty years of age. I sensed that I was a large portion of that, getting another opportunity. I had an inclination that I had been most of the way around the board and sent back to "go."

I watched Mace rest. He took a gander settled and untroubled. I wondered about the excellence of him. I winced at what I had missed. A large portion of my life had passed without him.

I kissed his shoulder and stimulated his side. "Mace," I said. "Wake up, infant."

He squinted and opened his eyes. "Never call me child again. It's one of my annoyances. I'm not a child. I'm a man. I scorn when sweethearts call each other child. It makes me wince."

"Is that what we are, darlings?"

"I accept that that is what is the issue here."

"At that point, awaken. I need my birthday present."

He moved onto his back, his face under mine. "I'm here. You previously got your present."

I kissed him. As it had such countless years back, lightning struck and thunder moved as our tongues lashed.

At the point when we broke, I guaranteed him I had loved constantly him. He guaranteed me the equivalent. "That is the thing that consistently and always implies," he reminded me.

We had gone far to go through the week in bed, however that is fundamentally what we did. We possessed a great deal of energy for which we needed to make up.

We had both improved at same sex. San Blas was mysterious. There was little we didn't do or, in any event, attempt.

The couple of times we dared to the sea shore, we either had intercourse in the water or surged back to our room, one of us so ravenous for the other that we were unable to pause. In one of our experiences in the water, it must be clear the thing we were doing. Mace was skimming on his back, his trunks off and covering his groin. I was remaining between his legs, holding them. I was within him as he professed to glide. I was unable to screw him, so he worked me with his muscles. When I pulled out and jacked my cum into the water, Mace was giggling so hard I dreaded he would suffocate.

Our last evening, we took a stroll on the sea shore. We were clasping hands. Mace, never one to dance around the issues, asked "What's next?"

"I figure you should separate from Juan and move to Denver."

"I'm not going to separate from Juan. What's more, I'm not going to move to Denver."

"You need to separate from Juan to wed me."

"Who said anything regarding wedding you?"

I was shocked. I thought we were both in a similar spot, unexpectedly. We were not.

We talked it through. As we talked, obviously Mace profoundly, genuinely love Juan. I was shocked.

We concluded Mace would reveal to Juan that we had reconnected and afterward leave it to him. In the event that Juan needed a separation, he would have one. In the event that he didn't, he would not, and Mace would keep on visiting Juan two or three times each year, except if and until Juan chose to re-visitation of the States. Mace and I would visit each other meanwhile.

It was not ideal, and it was not what I had anticipated. However, it was everything I might have, and I had no remaining to request more. I had relinquished that years back.

Mace announced back. Juan didn't need a separation. His folks had been hitched for what seems like forever, and he needed his kids' folks to be hitched for what seems like forever. Furthermore, paying little heed to where he was and what he was doing, he adored Mace. Obviously he did.

Juan was not excited I was back, however disclosed to Mace he was not amazed. He had accepted, sooner or later, I would acknowledge what I had missed and make a play. He was amazed just that it had taken me such a long time.

He didn't figure Mace would have the option to state no. He didn't know he would state indeed, but rather he was essentially certain he would state perhaps.

I traveled to San Diego all other fridaies. Mace traveled to Denver the ends of the week I was not in San Diego.

In the primary year we were back to us, Mace went to Bogota once at regular intervals. He was generally gone multi week. We didn't talk about Juan when he returned.

After his third outing, Mace disclosed to me Juan needed me to go along with him on the following excursion. I was incredulous.

"I think he needs to check whether there is a drawn out arrangement that works for everybody."

"There is. Separation and re-marriage."

"Not every person gets separated as effectively as you," Mace stated, ridiculing me.

"Ouch," I reacted, claiming not to be injured.

Mace and I traveled to Bogota together. Juan had a lovely metropolitan condo that he had acquired from his folks. Mace's sack went to Juan's room. My pack went to a subsequent room.

Andres and Camilo went along with us for supper. Just eleven months separated, they looked like indistinguishable, dazzling twins. They resembled the Colombian soccer player James, who had shaken the 2014 World Cup.

I knew through Mace that they were indistinguishable, closest companions the manner in which just indistinguishable twins normally are. He guessed that they would wed sisters or closest companions in a joint wedding, live nearby to one another, and have kids not long after one another. Andres could never cherish his better half like he adored Camilo, and Camilo could never adore his significant other the manner in which he adored Andres.

After Andres and Camilo got back to their quarters, we tidied up, Juan and Mace went to their room, and I went to mine. The hierarchy was being set up. Juan was peacocking, or so I thought.

I was practically sleeping when I heard a thump on my entryway. "Come in," I replied.

The entryway opened, and Juan and Mace remained there together. "We'd like you to go along with us," Mace said.

"Truly, kindly Juan added.

I was paralyzed by the thing they were proposing.

"It's the solitary way," Mace guaranteed me.

On the off chance that it was the lone way, at that point it was the lone way. I got a cushion and protected myself from them, similarly as I had such countless years before from Mace. They moved separated to allow me to pass. Mace got the pad as I did and threw it back on the bed.

Juan and Mace slipped their clothing off and went along with me in the bed. I had never had a three-way. When it was finished, I was unable to accept what I had been missing.

I viewed Juan and Mace kiss. I watched Mace work his way down Juan's bristly middle and take him in his mouth. Likely, I kissed Juan's delicate lips while Mace worked his dick. I was amazed by how he kissed me back.

I felt Mace move to my dick. I felt Juan work Mace around with the goal that Mace was in Juan's mouth and I was in Mace's mouth.

I worked Juan around so he was in my mouth.

Without examining it, we as a whole changed positions. We were all straight on, kissing, three tongues out and fighting. Juan was in the center, and he took Mace and me in each hand. Mace kissed Juan while I investigated his chest and stomach hair. Juan pulled my arm over his face and smelled my armpit.

"Juan likes smells," Mace murmured. "A great deal."

I covered my face in Juan's armpit and inhaled profoundly. "I see what he prefers," I murmured. I sucked Juan's areola and afterward turned my face to his dick. I laid my head on his midsection and took his dick in my mouth. I wanted to make him come. I worked him hard as he and Mace kept on kissing. I felt him buck and come and afterward felt him discharge into my mouth. I went to the base and gulped all he had.

I heard "Mark, I need you to screw me." It didn't come from Mace.

I moved between Juan's legs. Mace gave me a condom and lube. I applied both and slipped within Juan while he and Mace kept on kissing.

Mace moved behind me and began kneading my cheeks and afterward eating my butt. I heard the tear of foil and the flip of a cover. I felt cold fluid and afterward a hard dick. Mace planned to screw me while I screwed Juan.

It was more troublesome than it seemed like it ought to have been. From the start, I continued sneaking out of Juan. Mace dominated. "You move," he said. "Go moderate, at that point accelerate." He held my hips as I slid to and fro on him and all through Juan. I got into cadence. I got woozy. Juan took himself in his grasp and shared the cadence. We as a whole met up, Mace and I filling condoms and Juan covering his chest and stomach.

We were in Bogota seven days. We went through consistently and each day like we had gone through that first evening.

I went with Mace to Bogota like clockwork for the following two years. We spent each visit like we had spent that first visit.

Epilog

Andres and Camilo graduated and followed their dad to UCSD's Medical School. Juan followed his children back to the States, back to his home with Mace in San Diego.

Mace quit visiting Denver all other weekends. I kept on visiting San Diego. We as a whole contributed to add a second floor to their home. The whole floor was an expert suite. It had a custom bed that effortlessly obliged three grown-ups. It additionally had three restrooms and three stroll in storerooms. At long last, it had a general perspective on the gulch and a deck from which to appreciate that see.

It was not what I expected when I was more youthful, envisioning my life. For hell's sake, it was not what I expected when Mace deplaned in San Blas, reacting to my amazing signal.

On the off chance that I needed to take Juan to get Mace, at that point it was a simple choice for me. At long last.

Regardless, I developed to adore Juan. Dislike I cherished Mace, yet I never adored anybody like I cherished Mace. I never would.

We were cheerful when we were together. Mace was consistently in the center. He was the support. Juan didn't play appear to mind, and neither did I.

We were not equivalents. Juan and I never acted without Mace. Juan and Mace regularly acted without me. Infrequently, Mace and I acted without Juan, regularly just if Juan was away.

Following five years of flying to and fro, I resigned and moved to San Diego to be with Mace. Also, with Juan.

It was obvious to me that the hierarchy remained. It was the Juan and Mace story. I was separated, circling around them. At the point when I stirred in the evening, Mace was typically nestled into to Juan, his hand resting in Juan's chest hair. The bind that bound Mace to me remained, yet it was not close to as solid as the tie that bound Juan and Mace. I had been self-important to figure I could waltz once more into Mace's life and fix what he had gone through many years doing.

Without declaration or conversation, I moved out of the Master Suite. There was sufficient space for us all, however insufficient Mace for me. I got just what Juan didn't need or need.

Decisions have outcomes. I had flubbed the lone two choices I confronted that made a difference, the primary when Mace found out if I would wed him, and the second when Randy said essentially "simply give the signal." I would have offered anything to go back as expected, to murmur in my more youthful self's ear that what my more youthful self idea made a difference didn't, that all that made a difference was love and the strength it gave, that when you discover genuine romance, you should clutch it for dear life, regardless. I was unable to time travel. I could just arrangement with the outcomes of my decisions. As I lay alert around evening time, alone in my different room, I pondered about what may have been, the expressions of George Jones' "Decisions" repeated in my ears. I was living and passing on with the decisions I had made.

In the event that I had been more grounded, I would have proceeded onward and out of their home. In any case, I was getting old, and the personal minutes we as a whole shared - over supper, on a stroll, around a fire - were more critical to me now. Or then again so I persuaded myself.

I additionally stayed frail. I didn't have the solidarity to leave Mace once more.

Each once in for some time, I discovered Mace watching me. In those minutes, when every other person retreated and it was he just he and I, I knew, or trusted I knew, he was thinking about the thing I was continually pondering . . . What if.

Andres and Camilo are the two specialists. They are each hitched to light haired, blue looked at American ladies. They live nearby to one another. They each have two young men, ages 4 and 2. Every one of them four call me Uncle Mark. The hierarchy endures.

Chet and Charles are still attached. They are in the Sudan, attempting step by step to free Africa from defilement and to save the world. They will come up short, yet they will pass on difficult. Cheerfully.

They have embraced six vagrants, four of whom are HIV+. They are both enormous hearted, submitted communists, and they will continue to go inasmuch as there are vagrants, particularly vagrants with "the hiv."

With the assistance of different governments, we store their lives. We have been surprisingly fruitful. One Doctor and two legal counselors mean we have cash to consume. We send it to Africa to save vagrants as opposed to consuming it.

I visit Chet and Charles for a month each colder time of year. A year ago, Mace tagged along. Juan was taking the young men and their kids to Colombia to meet or visit his more distant family. Colombia had progressed significantly, however not so far that was welcome in Juan's family.

For a month in the Sudan, it was simply Mace and I, similar to it was such a long time ago in that back room on Tulane, when I had no clue about what the forms and states of "consistently and everlastingly" could or would be or could or would mean.

As we talked and strolled, inseparably, I felt like the "Mace and Mark" story was the fundamental storyline, as Juan was the optional character, not me. It was the most loved month of my life, me, Mace, and my child. I had an inclination that I was carrying on with the everyday routine I ought to have been experiencing from the beginning, if just I had not been powerless.

Yet, I had been frail. Also, my shortcoming had cost me.

On the off chance that lone I had not been frail, Mace and I would have had a coexistence. A full life.

On the off chance that solitary I had not been frail, Mace and I would have youngsters together. Our kids.

On the off chance that solitary I had not been feeble, I would have Mace to myself as I entered the dusk of my life. I would have him, and just him, to hold my hand and to shepherd me home.

Assuming just . . . .

Those two basic words, those three basic syllables, those six straightforward letters . . . . They frequent me and will keep on frequenting me until nothing can frequent me any longer.

Up to that point, I will know.

Assuming just, the lightning would have remained in the jug.

Assuming just, consistently and everlastingly would have been for eternity.

Assuming just . . .

CPSIA information can be obtained
at www.ICGtesting.com
Printed in the USA
BVHW081143140521
607268BV00002B/774